This book belongs to:

....

....

This book

belongs to:

MY BOOK OF

SILLY

STORIES

MY BOOK OF

SILLY

STORIES

Written by
NICOLA BAXTER

Illustrated by
SASCHA LIPSCOMB

This is a Parragon Book
First published in 2000

Parragon
Queen Street House
4 Queen Street
Bath BA1 1HE, UK

ISBN 0-75253-510-2

Produced for Parragon by
Nicola Baxter
PO Box 215
Framingham Earl
Norwich NR14 7UR

Designed by Amanda Hawkes

Printed in Italy

Contents

The Flying Pig

Many pigs are happy with a normal, snuffling, munching kind of life. They may moan about the size of their dinners. They may wish they had more wallowing time. But on the whole they are happy being pigs.

Puggle wasn't like that. Even as a piglet he yearned for something more. When his father introduced him, with a show of natural piggy pride, to the proper techniques for rootling out turnips, Puggle shook his little pink head.

"I might get my nose dirty," he said.

Puggle's father paused. He could hardly believe his ears. I mean, pigs *like* getting dirty, don't they? Nose, tummies, trotters and tails are regularly covered in mud. By comparison, rootling for turnips is a clean and tidy job. The older pig decided that he simply hadn't made himself clear.

"You see, son," he said, raising his voice a little and talking very slowly, "turnips are good to eat. Mmmm! Yummy! And in order to get them out of the ground, you have to shovel about with your snout, like this. Mmmnnfffmmm! See? It's not unpleasant. It's fun! It's something pigs are good at. Rootling, that is. Now, you have a go."

"No, thank you," said Puggle. He always had been a polite little pig.

Mr. Pig tried again. "It's not a case of 'No, thank you,' Puggle," he said, a little more sharply. "This is something that *all* pigs do. And you will do it too. In fact, you will do it now. Get rootling!"

Puggle knew the voice of command when he heard it, so he rootled. But he really cannot be said to have enjoyed it. And turnips have never been his favourite food from that day to this.

A very similar thing happened when Mrs. Pig tried to teach her son how to wallow really effectively in not-quite-wet-enough mud.

"You have to wiggle on your back a bit more," she explained, "which you don't have to do if the mud is really slurpy. Look, like this!"

And she wallowed very well.

"Now it's your turn, Puggle," she smiled. "This will be a real treat."

"But Puggle looked dubiously down at the puddle in front of his trotters.

"Must I?" he asked. "It doesn't seem very dignified, somehow."

"Dignified? Dignified? What on earth are you talking about?" squeaked his mother. "Wallowing is very dignified —for a pig. Who have you been talking to?"

Both Mr. and Mrs. Pig had a great fear of Undesirable Influences. By this they chiefly meant the sheep out in the meadow, who had nothing to do all day but gossip and who were quite likely to fill a young pig's head full of nonsense. Now that Mrs. Pig came to think about it, she felt sure that was what had happened. After all, sheep are always terribly nervous about getting their coats dirty. She gave her son a piece of her mind on the subject of sheep and their silliness and told him to run away and play so that she could wallow in peace.

Puggle was happy to escape into the farmyard. The sooner he could get back to his experiments, the better.

Yes, the reason that Puggle was not interested in rootling or wallowing was because he was *very* interested in flying. Ever since he had first looked up and seen the blue sky full of fluffy white clouds, he had longed to fly.

Later, when he was still a tiny piglet squiggling in the straw, he had been almost unbearably excited by the sight of a flock of swallows flying overhead. So animals could fly too! He couldn't wait to start flying himself.

Almost as soon as he could walk, Puggle was ready to fly. Except, of course, that there was a problem. He wasn't ready. No pig was ready.

"Mother," he asked one day, "when will my wings grow?"

Mrs. Pig heard "wings" but thought "tusks". The question didn't make any sense otherwise.

"You need to be a bit older, Puggle," she said, "and even then, not all pigs grow tusks. You must be patient."

Puggle was patient—for a week or two. Then he asked the question again. This time, there wasn't any doubt. Mrs. Pig frowned and paused in her munching.

"Wings? What wings?" she said. "Honestly, Puggle, you do have some extraordinary ideas. Pigs don't have wings, sweetheart."

"What, never ever?" asked Puggle. "Never, ever, ever?"

"Not ever," said Mrs. Pig firmly. "It's a silly idea, Puggle. Pigs are too ... er ... portly to fly. A nicely rounded pig couldn't get off the ground under his own steam however many wings he had."

Puggle was shattered. He had assumed that it was only a matter of time before he too could be soaring through the blue. It seemed he would have to explore other avenues.

A few days later, Puggle was lying miserably under a tree, when he happened to overhear a mother blackbird teaching her little ones how to fly. This was news to Puggle.

He had assumed that flying came naturally to a creature with wings. But as he listened to the blackbird mother giving careful instructions to her brood, he felt hope rising within him once again. If bird-brained blackbirds could learn to fly, surely a super-intelligent pig could do it, given enough thought and practice.

There followed several very painful days during which Puggle tried to launch himself off higher and higher objects. The feed trough incident only jolted his front trotters. The sty wall incident left him with a badly bumped bottom.

The sty roof attempt could have been much more serious, but it was luckily an excellent day for wallowing, and the many pigs who were doing so were quite plump and squashy—ideal material on which to land. Even so, Puggle's pride was badly dented and several elderly pigs took to their beds, suffering from shock.

Puggle thought long and hard about jumping from the tree where the baby birds had been practising. He certainly had the courage to try it, but he soon found that trotters were not ideal for climbing tree trunks. Once again, Puggle felt that his dreams had been crushed. He lay under the tree and moaned softly to himself (and that was only partly because of the badly bumped bottom).

Once again, it was a chance event that gave Puggle hope. High overhead, he heard a droning sound. It grew louder and louder and louder. A squirrel who lived in the trunk of the tree came hurtling through the branches, desperate to get back into her hole.

"What is it?" yelled Puggle, for the noise overhead was very loud now.

"It's an aeroplane," shouted the squirrel. "Haven't you ever seen one before? They're a real nuisance, especially when I'm trying to get my little ones to sleep. I can hardly hear myself think!"

Puggle waited a moment or two for the noise to die away, then he turned to the squirrel, who was preparing to leap off up the tree again, and begged for more information.

"But what is it?" he asked. "I mean, what is an aeroplane? I know that it flies and it makes a lot of noise. Is it an animal? Does it do anything else? Does it ever come to land?"

"I'm not completely sure," confessed the squirrel, anxious to be gone. "I don't think it's an animal. I think it's a machine, like a car. And I don't think it ever does land. I've never seen one on the ground. I think it drones about up there all the time."

But when the squirrel had gone, and Puggle had a chance to think, he felt more optimistic once again. You see, pigs are a lot cleverer than squirrels, and the squirrel had said that an aeroplane was like a car. Puggle knew that cars carried people. Wasn't it possible that aeroplanes carried people as well, only through the air instead of along the ground?

The more Puggle thought about it, the surer he felt that this was so. A few days later, his suspicions were confirmed when one of the farm children left a library book out on the grass. Puggle had nibbled the cover and chewed a couple of pages before he noticed that the pictures in the book were all of flying machines.

And the machines definitely had people in them. Certainly, they were strange people, with helmets and scarves and huge goggly eyes, but then people were strange anyway, in pig terms. Puggle looked very carefully at the pictures and was very sorry about the pages that were now inside him. He wished he could read the black squiggles. Nevertheless, Puggle went to sleep that night with a head buzzing with ideas. For the first time in a long while, flying seemed a real possibility.

The next morning, Puggle set to work to build his flying machine. It's surprising what you can find lying in the back of a barn if you look hard enough. Pretty soon, Puggle had assembled a large crate, a bicycle wheel, a plank of wood and lots of bits of binder twine to fix everything together. Trotters are not ideal for tying knots, but snouts are pretty good, so by the end of the day, Puggle had something that looked very like a plane.

At least, it had a cockpit and wings, and the bicycle wheel on the front looked a little bit like a propeller.

Puggle knew that it would be wise to get a good night's sleep before starting on his adventure. He wasn't, for one thing, quite sure how easy night flying was. But halfway to his sty, he turned around. This was too exciting to wait. If he was going to fly, he must do it now!

As the sun set behind the far fields, Puggle climbed into his flying machine. He thought hard about flying, but nothing happened. He peered over the edge of the cockpit but found he was still very near the ground. Nearer, in fact, than very near. As near as you can get. Once again, Puggle paused for thought.

Of course! A machine needed to make noise to work. Certainly the farmer's car and tractors made a terrible noise, and now he came to think of it, the aeroplane had made a truly deafening din.

"Brrrrrrrrrrmmmmm!" said Puggle. "Brrrrrmm! Brrrmm! BRRRRMMM!"

But nothing happened. The plane didn't so much as jiggle. It was as earthbound as a pig. And the pig on board was feeling his heart sink to his trotters once again. Sadly, he climbed out and set off for the sty.

Now Puggle was a fortunate young pig in many ways, and not only because he had such an enquiring mind. He also happened to be a particularly fine-looking pig, which is not surprising when you consider that both his parents had won prizes at the County Show.

A few days later, the farmer gave Puggle a very thorough wash (including parts he didn't even know he had) and brushed his trotters until they shone. Then he loaded the young pig, together with a sheep who looked as if she had been to the hairdresser's and a duck with astonishingly white feathers, into the back of his truck and set off for the local show ground. He felt pretty sure that Puggle at least would win a rosette.

Puggle rather enjoyed his wash and brush up. He liked the idea of seeing somewhere new, too. After all, it would keep his mind off the disappointments in his flying career.

Puggle did, indeed, do very well at the show. He won first prize and had a great many ladies in hats and men with monocles cooing over him. But later in the afternoon, while the judges were looking at the sheep, Puggle became rather bored. He lifted the latch of his crate with his clever little snout and set off to explore the show ground. He might have aroused some comment from the crowd if at that moment everyone had not been staring at the sky. A familiar noise was coming louder and louder above the throng.

Puggle couldn't see a thing among all the legs of the crowd. He climbed up on to a bale of straw and could hardly believe his eyes. There was a flying machine, flying low enough for him to be sure, yes, that there was a person inside. And the machine was looping-the-loop and doing all kinds of acrobatic stunts. Puggle's heart was thudding as the plane came in to land to the applause of the crowd. As the pilot jumped out on to the field, the spectators surged forward to meet him.

Why did no one notice a little pink shape flashing across the field? Why did no one notice when the engine of the plane throbbed into life again? Even when the plane began to move forward, slowly at first and then faster and faster, no one shouted. It was only when Puggle pulled the throttle right back and the engines roared into the loudest of life that the pilot, busy autographing programmes, yelled out, "My plane!"

It was too late. Puggle grinned and waved a careless trotter to the people who were getting smaller and smaller below him. He felt wonderful! It was just as good as he had known it would be. As he gained in confidence, he swooped and he swerved. He was born to fly and everyone could see it now.

Now Puggle was an extraordinary pig, but he was a pig all the same. He found himself steering towards his home.

Puggle looked down at the farm. It seemed very, very far away. His pigsty was a tiny dot in the corner of the farmyard. His feed trough was an even tinier dot. Puggle felt a pang. It hit him somewhere between his ribs in a place that he liked to keep full of something tasty. It occurred to him that several hours had passed since breakfast. Exciting hours. Amazing hours. But hours completely lacking in any kind of pig-pleasing nourishment.

Puggle throttled back and prepared to land. In the great celestial struggle between flying and eating, there's really no contest...

The Very Hungry Hat

Algernon F. Addlethwaite was not a fashionable man. Passers-by who glanced at his clothes either shuddered or leant faintly against a lamp-post. Most people averted their eyes from his favourite knee-length shorts, striped socks and clogs ensemble. You probably would yourself.

But things took a desperate turn for the worse when Algernon decided he needed a hat. His hat choice was much, much more unfortunate than any of his other clothing selections.

You see, the hat in question was a very hungry hat. It liked to eat hair. As you walked about in the hat, you might feel a slight and not-unpleasant tingling around your head. When you took the hat off, you would be totally and utterly bald. Some people to whom this happened decided to keep the hat on all the time to hide their shiny heads, but that was an even worse mistake than buying the hat in the first place. You see, without hair to nibble, the hat had a terrible tendency to snack on ears instead.

On the day that Algernon F. Addlethwaite met the hat, he had, in fact, been thinking about hair. He lived with his aunt, Agatha Addlethwaite. That morning at breakfast, she looked up at her nephew and shuddered.

"Algie," she said, "you must get your hair cut. It's a disgrace. I can hardly concentrate on my eggs and toast with all that flippety-floppety stuff at the other end of the table." Aunt Agatha's voice, although quavery, was surprisingly firm for a woman in her nineties.

Algernon made a vague sound in the back of his throat. It might have meant anything. He had very little intention of getting his hair cut.

Aunt Agatha, however, had very little intention of dropping the subject.

"Don't make that vague sound in the back of your throat," she bellowed. "It might mean anything. I'll make you an appointment with Signor Alfonso."

Within minutes, the deed was done. Signor Alfonso, who kept Aunt Agatha's hair in its gleaming lilac loveliness, would expect Algernon at a quarter to ten. A taxi would call for Algernon at half past nine. There would be no shilly-shallying, dilly-dallying or other attempts to get out of it.

Algernon felt resigned. When Aunt Agatha made up her mind to do something, it was usually easiest to go along with it. In truth, Algernon did not care very much what happened to his hair or any other part of his appearance. His mind was always full of his real passion in life, which was the study of carnivorous plants. Unfortunately, Aunt Agatha would not allow them in the house. Despite her nephew's assurances, she felt sure that one of them might devour her Pekinese, Mr. Dipples. And Mr. Dipples, I'm afraid, was rather more important to the old lady than Algernon F.

Algernon F. Addlethwaite climbed into the taxi that would deliver him to Signor Alfonso and waved vaguely at his aunt. He was busy wondering if he could smuggle a specimen of *Dionaea muscipula* (Venus flytrap to you and me) into his bedroom. The growing conditions there were perfect. In fact, the whole house would make a wonderful home for the collection of plants that Algernon dreamed of one day making. Every day, he went to the Botanical Gardens and stood for hours watching unwary flies meeting their doom, but it wasn't the same as being able to do it in your own home.

"Signor Addlethwaite!" Alfonso was on the pavement to greet Algernon. The transformation was about to begin.

How long does it take you to get your hair cut? Ten minutes? Fifteen? Twenty, perhaps? When I tell you that Algernon F. Addlethwaite was in Signor Alfonso's number one chair for two hours and seventeen minutes, you will know that the Algie who entered his pink and perfumed premises was not the Algie who wandered out of them.

Signor Alfonso had gone to town. There were curls, ringlets even. There was a flicked-up bit at the front. There was a dangling-down bit at the back. And there was the colour. Not exactly blue. Not exactly purple. Not exactly magenta. Signor Alfonso called it "Midnight in Milan". "Nightmare in Milan" was nearer the mark. You can imagine, I'm sure, that Algernon crept from shop and ran at once to find something to cover his head.

Wrong! With his mind on the rain forests of deepest Brazil and the plants that are found there, Algernon said, "Thank you. It looks fine!" to Signor Alfonso and strolled off down the road without a care in the world. Several unwary pedestrians, however, walked into shop windows or traffic lights at the sight of him and had to receive medical treatment for minor grazes and suspected halucinations.

It was not until he had taken up his usual position in one of the glasshouses at the Botanical Gardens that Algernon began to suspect that something was wrong. Not a single fly approached any of the plants, but Algernon soon became aware of a strange buzzing in his ears. There was a tickling at the back of his neck, too. It took him half an hour to realize what was happening. There were no flies meeting their doom in the flowerbeds because every fly for miles around was having a party in Algernon's new hairstyle. There was clearly something about "Midnight in Milan" and its curious smell that was a magnet for minibeasts.

Most people would be horrified to find insects in their hair. Algernon was not worried at all. But he *was* horrified to find no insects settling on his beloved plants. He knew that action was necessary and must be taken at once.

Moving at a speed that would have astonished his Aunt Agatha, Algernon hurried back to the High Street, his head humming inside and out. Signor Alfonso must put this right at once.

But Signor Alfonso's salon door was firmly closed. "Closed for holidays. Back in 3 weeks." was written on it in the kind of swirly writing that is very hard to read.

Three weeks! Algernon gasped and stared. Three weeks without being able to look at his precious plants? Three weeks without being able to see a single fly crawling slowly towards destruction? It simply wasn't possible.

Algernon was not a stupid man. His brains worked just as well as yours. It was simply that most of the time they were thinking about carnivorous plants instead of sensible things like soccer and sandwiches. It is at moments of crisis that we have to think fast. Algernon thought very fast indeed. Parts of his hairstyle began to wilt in the heat of the thinking that was going on just below them. In seconds, Algernon had made his decision and was off, running down the High Street as if his life depended on it. (More pedestrians had difficulty with lamp-posts and litter bins. Algernon didn't notice.)

Algernon rushed into the nearest Gentleman's Outfitters and demanded to see hats.

"Hats, Sir?" asked the assistant, looking Algernon up and down with an unfriendly air.

"Yes, hats. I don't mind what they look like."

"I can imagine, Sir." The assistant had drawn his own conclusions from his customer's clothes and coiffure.

"I'm in a hurry!" cried Algernon, but the assistant did not move.

"Unfortunately, Sir, we are between hats at the moment. Our winter stock is sold out and our summer stock will be arriving next week. I could offer you an eye-shade or an umbrella."

"No, no! That won't do!" Algernon rushed from the shop and headed down the street again. It was the same story in all the men's clothing shops he entered. It was a nightmare!

Algernon wasn't proud. He didn't care about anything except his plants. He plunged into Bella's Boutique and asked to see ladies' hats. The one in the window would be fine.

It was Bella herself who delicately extracted the hat from the window. It was an enormous confection of feathers and flowers. "It would be much better, sir," she said, "if the lady came in and tried on the hat herself."

"It's for me," said Algernon, leaning forwards to take the hat.

"For a fancy dress party? For a play? For a joke?" enquired Bella, taking a step backwards.

"To keep the flies off my hair!" cried Algernon. "Quickly, please!"

Bella looked at Algernon's head a little more closely ... and screamed. She had not noticed the creeping and crawling that was taking place just a few feet from her nose. Algernon fled from the shop. Bella was not a woman to harbour insects of any kind among her millinery.

Poor Algernon! His increasing air of desperation did not help. Several shops showed him the door before he had even explained what he wanted. Two assistants fainted and one called the police. Not a hat, not a headscarf, not a helmet could he buy in the whole town.

Then he found the very hungry hat.

It was lying on the pavement. It might be more accurate to say that it was lying in wait on the pavement, but poor Algernon did not know this. He simply saw the answer to all his problems and picked it up. To do him justice, he looked up and down the street, in case the owner of the hat was even at that moment on his way to find it. But there was no one – only a bald man holding his ears climbing on to a bus. Algernon clapped the hat on to his head and hurried back to the Botanical Gardens, where he spent a very pleasant afternoon indeed watching several flies and an unwary beetle wiggling their last.

It was a soothed and happy Algernon F. Addlethwaite who made his way home at the end of the afternoon. The hours with Alfonso and the horrors of hopeless hat-buying were all forgotten. He hurried into the house.

Aunt Agatha was already at the table in the dining room.

"Algernon!" she cried. "You are late! Come and sit down at once, and for goodness sake take off that hat! Where are your manners?"

Algernon took off his hat.

Aunt Agatha fainted into her soup.

After that, things happened very quickly. As Aunt Agatha came round and gazed up at Algernon's entirely bald head, the hat, bored and, let's face it, hungry, scuttled across the floor. It had sighted something hairy sleeping in the corner.

Aunt Agatha was a woman of strong character. She tried hard to accept the sight of Algernon at the other end of the supper table. She assumed that his shining head was the result of Signor Alfonso's creative hairdressing. It was unusual, certainly. It was not attractive. But it was better than flippety floppety hair across the table.

"Well, dear, I'll be off to bed now," said Aunt Agatha, rising from the table. "Come along, Mr. Dipples."

The Pekinese trotted across to his mistress. Aunt Agatha let out a piercing scream. "Algernon! You have brought one of your horrible plants into the house. Look! Just look at poor Mr. Dipples!" The dog, too, was completely bald.

Aunt Agatha did not stay in that house another night. She packed her bags and left, with Mr, Dipples discreetly wrapped in a shawl.

Today, Algernon F. Addlethwaite lives happily surrounded by carnivorous plants. He no longer needs to leave the house, so there are far fewer accidents in town involving pedestrians and lamp-posts. And the hat? Well, who knows? But if you should happen to see it, I have one important piece of advice. DON'T PUT IT ON!

The Best Birthday Cake

Amanda Sarah Jane Jones was looking forward to her birthday party. She had invited everyone in her class at school and given her parents strict instructions about the food, the music, the balloons and the party bags they should arrange. Her mother and father, seeing a very determined glint in her eye and her foot poised to stamp, had hastily agreed to all her ideas. It was, after all, her birthday. It was also six months away, but Amanda Sarah Jane was the kind of girl who believed in starting her campaigns early.

In the months that followed her demands, Amanda went to the birthday parties of several of her friends. If they had giant balloons, she soon told her long-suffering parents she needed super-giant balloons. If they had two tasty kinds of sandwiches, she ordered three kinds. Her party would be better than anyone's.

But as the weeks passed, and she went to even more parties, Amanda began to see that her plans had a big hole in them, and it was a hole right in the middle where a birthday cake should be. Polly, who had her own pony, had a special cake in the shape of her beloved Velvet. Akiko's father made her a cake shaped like an enormous kite, with liquorice strings and candy bows. Xavier, whose birthday was near Hallowe'en, had a cake shaped like a pumpkin – and it was hollow and had a candle inside.

Amanda became very thoughtful.

About a month before her birthday, she tried to make her parents understand the importance of this feature of her party.

"You see," she said, "the cake is the centre of everything. It has to be carried in near the end so that everyone can sing Happy Birthday to me and be amazed."

"Be amazed?" asked her father. "By what exactly?"

"By the cake!" said Amanda. This was going to be harder than she thought.

"Are people amazed by cakes?" asked her mother. "I don't think I've ever been amazed by a cake. Have you, Pete?"

"I've been amazed by rock cakes," said her husband with some feeling. "I cracked a tooth on your mother's."

"My mother is an excellent cook!" Amanda's mother sounded frosty. "She taught me everything I know."

There was an unpleasant silence as both Amanda and her father tried to think of something tactful to say. But Mrs. Jones was going on.

"I was thinking of one of my big chocolate cakes, but with candles on top," she said. "That would be okay, wouldn't it?"

Amanda's father exchanged a glance with his daughter. "I guess it wouldn't be *amazing*," he said. "Maybe we should buy one this time. They do them for all the popular TV characters now, you know."

"Well!" cried Mrs. Jones.

"No!" cried Amanda.

"There," said her mother, "I knew my chocolate cake would be fine."

"No!" Amanda felt the moment had come to be firm. "I don't want a chocolate cake and I don't want a bought cake. I want a special cake that no one else has ever had. And I want it to be huge. I was thinking that a Princess's Palace would be good, with flags from the turrets, lights at the windows and music coming out of it."

"Flags?"

"Lights?"

"Music?"

Amanda's parents looked bemused.

"You could order it from that shop in the Mall," Amanda explained, making her voice patient and friendly as if she was talking to two-year-olds.

"We'll see," said her mother. "It's not a bad idea. I'll be very busy with the other food. It would be good to have the cake taken out of my hands."

On Saturday, the whole family went shopping, and Amanda made sure they "happened" to pass the cake shop she had in mind.

"Oh look," she said brightly. "We might as well go and see about my cake since we're here." And in they went.

The shop assistant began by talking to Amanda's parents, but it soon became clear who was in charge, so she and Amanda had a long discussion about the details of the cake, and the assistant really entered into the spirit of the thing.

"How about fluorescent icing?" she said, "so that you could turn the lights out when the cake was brought in? And we could make smoke come out of the base, like mist, you know, to add to the air of fairytale magic."

Amanda agreed to the fluorescent icing but turned down the mist on the grounds that it might get out of hand and hide the wonderful cake. Eventually, she and the assistant had everything settled between them.

"I'll send an estimate of the price to you, shall I?" she asked Amanda's parents. "It's only a formality, but it helps to sort these things out in advance."

"That's a good idea," said Mr. Jones.

A week passed, and Amanda spent quite a lot of it telling her friends at school about the amazing birthday cake she had ordered. She didn't give any details because she wanted it to be a surprise, but she dropped hints about hugeness and special effects that made her friends turn emerald with envy.

But the on Saturday morning, as the family sat down to breakfast, Amanda's father began to open the mail. All of a sudden, he turned pale and clutched his chest with a strangled gasp.

"Pete, what is it? Amanda, call an ambulance!" cried her mother, but Mr .Jones waved a feeble hand to stop her.

"It's th-th-the estimate f-f-from the c-c-cake shop," he stuttered. "Look!"

Mrs Jones looked ... and had to sit down. "It must be a joke," she said and hurried to the telephone.

Five minutes later, it was clear that the extraordinarily enormous amount of money in the estimate was not a joke.

"I will *not* remortgage the house!" cried Mr. Jones dramatically.

Mrs. Jones was even more heroic. "You just tell me exactly what you want, darling," she told her daughter, "and I'll make it for you, even if I have to work night and day."

Amanda felt doubtful. She looked doubtful, too. But she could see there was very little choice. She began to outline her cherished plans.

A week before the party, Mrs. Jones rolled up her sleeves and started work.

"Would you like me to help?" asked her husband, putting his head around the kitchen door.

"No!" cried Mrs. Jones, thinking of a truly disastrous egg-boiling incident.

"No!" cried Amanda, thinking of the exploding sardines episode.

As Mr. Jones slunk away, Amanda and her mother began mixing truly huge quantities of ingredients. Every pan and bowl in the kitchen was called into service. The cooker only just took the strain, as batch after batch of mixture was cooked. Several layers of the cake were carried next door for Mrs. Mason to cook. Pretty soon the whole kitchen was filled with cooling cakes, while an exhausted Mrs. Jones flopped against the sink.

"Tomorrow," she said, "we'll get started on assembling it. Don't, whatever you do, let the dog into the kitchen!" For she could hear Ruffles whining at the door, his nose tickled by the tasty smell of cakes – dozens of them – cooking and cooling only a few feet away.

Early next morning the whole family began the task of putting the cake together. This time Mr. Jones was allowed to help, for he claimed to have engineering experience. Mrs. Jones privately suspected that this consisted of mending his bike when he was six, but she said nothing.

Mr. Jones' first contribution was an enormous board to place on the kitchen table, for the cake was much too big for any plate in the house. Mrs. Jones covered the board with foil and Amanda went round afterwards smoothing it out, even the parts that wouldn't be seen. She wanted everything to be perfect, after all. Then the building could begin.

It took all day to place one piece of cake on top of another. The parts were glued together with strawberry jam, and some were cut out to resemble towers, battlements and a grand staircase at the front. Amanda was the architect. Mrs. Jones did the precise cutting. Mr. Jones stood on a stepladder to position the turrets at the very top.

When the whole thing was finished, the Jones family stood back to admire it.

"That turret isn't straight," said the architect critically. "And the steps are wonky, too."

"It will settle overnight," said Mr. Jones airily. "And the icing will cover up a multitude of sins ... I mean, the icing will transform it completely."

Once again, Ruffles was banished to the hall and the doors were firmly shut. The cake was left in the darkness.

It was an early start again for the Jones family next day. Gallons and gallons of icing had to be mixed. Mr. Jones brightly suggested using the washing machine, but his wife's expression warned him not to pursue the matter.

The plan was for the icing to be the palest, prettiest pink, but the stuff that colours icing is very, very strong. Mr. Jones, measuring it out with a tablespoon instead of a teaspoon, managed to create a bowl of the brightest magenta icing you have ever seen. It looked revolting.

"I think white would be much more elegant," said Amanda firmly, hiding the bottle of pink stuff under the sink. She couldn't bear any more accidents to her wonderful cake.

Icing the cake was the trickiest part so far. Mrs. Jones tried spreading it very, very gently with a knife. Amanda tried dribbling it on with a spoon. Mr. Jones experimented with a throw-it-at-the-cake-and-see-if-it-sticks technique, which nearly demolished the north turret. Amanda had to confiscate his bowl of icing and instruct him on making little silver flags instead.

By the middle of the afternoon, with the cake only half iced, conditions in the kitchen became unbearable. It was partly because Mr. Jones was sulking over his flag-making. It was partly because Mrs. Jones was getting back-ache trying to reach the top of the cake. It was partly because Amanda kept checking on both her parents. But it was mostly because Ruffles would not stop whining outside the door. Even an extra-large bowl of doggy chunks didn't subdue him. The shut door made him absolutely sure that the family was having a good time without him, and he wasn't happy about it.

Mrs Jones turned on the radio to drown out the sounds. Ruffles stopped whining and started howling. The family found whining was better, but Mr. Jones was so desperate he stuffed a couple of bits of cake into his ears to try to shut it out. Don't try this at home. It doesn't work and it means you have crumbs on your collars for weeks afterwards.

It was almost midnight when the icing was finished at last. Amanda and her parents staggered up to bed, praying they never saw another cake as long as they lived. And Ruffles, still shut out of the kitchen, chewed the stair carpet in disgust.

The next morning, although all of them felt rather queasy at the sight of the cake, the Jones family began the final decorations. The party was at two o'clock, so everything had to be ready by then. Amanda positioned the flags (her Dad had to hold her up) and painted windows and doors with the famous fluorescent icing.

Mrs. Jones carefully put candles all around the base. Mr. Jones was in charge of the electronics. There were fairy lights to fix and the tiny radio to slide into a special hole in the side to play princess music when the big moment came.

At last everything was completely ready. Amanda stepped back and looked at her cake. There had been times over the last few days when she had wished she had never thought of it, but now she saw that it had all been worth it.

"Now keep all the doors shut," said Mrs Jones, as she rushed about, getting all the other elements of the party ready. "We don't want a disaster with Ruffles at the last moment." Ruffles made his feelings known in the usual way.

By half past one, Amanda was in her party dress and blowing up the last balloon. She had butterflies in her stomach and almost everywhere else. She had never felt so nervous. Even her parents entering races at Sports Day wasn't as worrying as this.

At seven minutes past two exactly, the first guests began to arrive. Ruffles, as a special treat, was allowed to join in the fun. The party got underway. Everything was just as wonderful as Amanda had planned. And the main attraction was yet to come.

By five o'clock, it was already dark. In the kitchen, Mr. and Mrs. Jones peered at the list of instructions their daughter had given them. Slowly, the hands of the clock clicked into place. It was time to carry in the cake!

"On my count," said Mr. Jones. "One, two, three, lift!" He was glad he had called in the neighbours to help. Two people could never have lifted the monster cake. The Masons and the Jones shuffled towards the door, the cake swaying between them. But two feet from the door a huge problem became clear. Width of cake: four feet five inches. Width of door: two feet ten inches. Result: disaster!

"Wait! Wait!" cried Mr. Jones. "Let me think!"

"Be quick!" cried Mrs. Jones. "I can't hold this for much longer!"

"The french windows! We can carry it around the outside of the house!" gasped her husband.

Mrs. Jones looked at him in frank astonishment. Yes, it would work! It was a good idea! "Everyone take four paces to the left!" she called.

Swaying dangerously, the cake was edged through the large kitchen window. It was not an easy task, but the team was not going to be beaten now. The Masons balanced the cake on the window sill as the Jones rushed around through the back door to take up the other side.

Then the cake was on the move again, slowly tottering down the path at the side of the house and round to the french windows in the party room.

"Can we come in?" called Mr. Jones. It was a signal. When Amanda heard the call, she was to turn off the lights so that the cake could make its grand entrance. At the same time, Mr. Jones nudged the switch on the battery (he had positioned it so he could reach it with his nose!) to turn on the fairy lights and the music. Mr. Mason, very cleverly, managed to open the doors with his bottom.

"Happy birthday to you!
Happy birthday to you…"

As the singing began and the doors swung open, a terrifying noise came from the party room.

"*Yaaaaaaarrrroooooooow!*" Ruffles, seeing the cake he had been so tantalized by all week, leapt forward with a howl of joy. Mr. Mason, seeing something furry with gleaming eyes flying towards him in the dark, crumpled to his knees with a cry of terror. The cake, jiggling like something alive, slid with a terrible inevitability on to the carpet —upside down.

Amanda turned on the lights when she heard the sickening thud. A mountain of cake and jam and icing filled the centre of the room. The fairy lights had been buried, but they somehow gave an eerie glow to the whole mess. Somewhere deep inside the cake, the radio was playing the Dance of the Sugar Plum Fairy.

Mr. Jones took one look at the musical Matterhorn and fled into the garden, falling over the fence in his hurry.

Amanda opened her mouth to cry and found something very much like a laugh coming out. After all that work. After all that planning. After all that...

The party guests stood like statues with their mouths open. They had been to pirate parties and fairy parties and cowboy parties. Never in their wildest dreams had they thought of holding a flying-cake party!

Mrs. Jones, worn out with days of work on the cake, could think only of the radio. Was strawberry jam even now glooping into its inner workings? She lost her head completely.

"A special prize to the first one to find the radio!" she cried, and twenty gleeful children and one excited dog leaped forward, howling with delight.

What else is there to say? The radio was found—eventually. The room was cleaned—eventually. Nineteen very happy and very sticky children went home, and one happy and very sticky child went up to bed with a blissful smile on her face.

"Thanks, Mum. Thanks, Dad," she said sleepily. "It wasn't what I planned but it was a party everyone will talk about for ever. And the cake was really *really* ... amazing!"

The Lion and the Zebra

Long ago on the dusty plains of Africa, there lived a lion who was lazy. Now, most lions are lazy—it's the lionesses who do all the work—but this one barely moved at all. He lay all day in the long grass below a spiky tree, snacking on the treats the lionesses brought him and watching the world go by.

One day, what went by was another lion. He was a young, handsome, lively lion who tossed his head in an attractive way and growled politely as he passed the lazy lion. Unfortunately, that one was too lazy even to roar back.

The lazy lion was not the only one to notice the newcomer. Several gazelles wandered off to what they thought was a safer distance. The vultures hunched their shoulders and hoped for a fight. But the lionesses noticed even more. They hurried over to the waterhole and had a meeting.

"We all know why we're here," said the eldest lioness. "Do we need to discuss this, ladies?"

"I say we vote with our feet," said a younger lioness. "I don't believe he would even notice we were gone."

"Sad but true," said her cousin. "I've known that lion for twenty years, and he's not going to change now. Let's leave him to it."

"Excuse me," said a very young and tender-hearted niece. "But will he be all right? I was thinking of food, you know."

"That's a good question," replied her aunt. "But he has claws, he has teeth, he has all the equipment he needs to live perfectly well. If he gets hungry, he has no one to blame but himself. Are we ready?"

They were. With one accord, the lionesses packed their bags and set off after the passing lion.

It was two days before the lazy lion realized they were gone. He woke one morning with an empty feeling deep down where his growl came from and he looked around for someone to do something about it. The dusty plain seemed strangely empty. There were zebras. There were giraffes. There were the usual herds of gazelles. But there was no one who looked as if they might be about to bring breakfast. The lazy lion grunted for a while and shut his eyes again. Perhaps after another little sleep, someone would turn up.

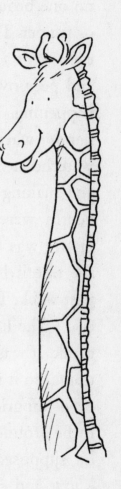

But another whole day passed and no one brought him any breakfast, lunch or supper. The lion began to feel faint. He even went so far as to raise his great head and peer over the grass to see what was happening. Nothing was happening. A happy warthog was wallowing in the waterhole. A gazelle was having a baby and making a lot of noise about it. Two zebras were comparing their stripes. A giraffe was eating the very last leaf from the tree it had been snacking on for the past week. There was no food in sight.

The lion lay down again and had a think. It wasn't something he was used to doing, so it was hard work and made him even hungrier. The lionesses didn't seem to be around. They might be on holiday, he supposed, but they usually let him know and stocked up his larder if they were going away. They might all be ill, but he thought he would have heard moaning if so. Could they, horror of horrors, all have met a dreadful end? It didn't seem very likely. Could they have been zapped by zebras or wiped our by warthogs? No, that didn't seem likely at all. Very, very slowly, the lion faced up to the fact that the lionesses had simply left, and left without leaving anything behind.

By the following morning, after he had dragged himself to the waterhole for a drink, the lion was beginning to feel light headed. It made thinking even harder.

Once again he gazed out over the dusty plain. The gazelles were gambolling, including the new one. The zebras were nibbling and nuzzling. The giraffes seemed to be dancing, and doing it rather well. No food.

But wait a minute. A dim memory of being a cub came into the lion's mind. When the lionesses brought him food, it often had hooves on. Very occasionally, it had a stripy outside. Didn't he remember something about lions eating *animals*? He had been looking at food all the time and not realizing it! All would be well!

The lazy lion lumbered to his feet and set off after the nearest animal, which happened to be a gazelle. Nearer and nearer he padded, puffing now with the exertion. Thirty feet ... twenty feet ... ten feet. This was easier than he had thought. But at just that moment, the gazelle

looked up, a surprised expression on her face. The gasping lion tried to look as if he meant business. He hunched himself up and got ready to spring. But while he was thinking about it, the gazelle giggled and scampered away—much, much faster than the lion could manage.

After another attempt on a gazelle, an unfortunate encounter with a warthog and a look of disdain from a giraffe, the lion began to panic. It was clear to him that catching food was not as easy as he had imagined. He became dimly aware that he could have been more grateful when the lionesses brought him tasty treats. What on earth was he going to do?

As he thought about things, the lion wandered across the grasslands, feeling fainter by the second. At last, exhausted and as empty as he had ever been, he slumped down for a rest.

"Hey! That's my place!" called a high-pitched voice. "What do you think you're doing?"

It was a zebra. A rather fat and tasty-looking zebra. The lion looked up wearily and then stared a little more carefully. This zebra was only a few feet away. The lion narrowed his eyes.

And the zebra burst out laughing. "You've got to be joking! Thinking of eating me? You'd have to catch me first! I've been watching you. You couldn't catch a sleeping hippo! Don't think that I'll be your dinner, mate. Oh, no!"

"I'm glad someone thinks it's funny," growled the lion. "But I don't think I can go on much longer. I'd be very grateful for some advice. Naturally, I wouldn't dream of trying to eat someone who was helping me."

The zebra stamped his hooves for a minute or two.

"All right," he said. "I'll do what I can, but you put zebras right off your menu, mate. I mean, right off."

The lion agreed, and the zebra sat down beside him.

"See, you've got to go for the weak ones. Baby gazelles are good. They can't run as fast as their parents. And sick old warthogs aren't bad, either, but I should think you'd get indigestion."

"But," the lion furrowed his regal brow, "that's not a very *nice* thing to do, is it? I mean, catching little youngsters and elderly chaps. It doesn't seem right. I don't think I could bring myself to do it."

"Then you've only got one choice, mate," said the zebra. "You'll have to become a vegetarian, like me. There's plenty of grass about and leaves, too, if you can reach them."

"I suppose I could give it a go," said the lion. "I'm so hungry now I could eat almost anything … except zebras, of course. Show me how you do it."

The zebra looked at him as if he was touched by the sun. Who needs to be shown how to eat? But the lion looked genuinely confused, so the zebra obligingly got up and chomped a mouthful of grass. The lion staggered to his feet and had a go.

But after two minutes, he flopped down again, licking his sore lips.

"It's no good," he said. "My teeth just aren't made for this nibbling and chomping. I'm more of a tearing and chewing sort of animal."

"That's what I'd heard," said the zebra grimly, thinking of an aunt of his who had gone missing under suspicious circumstances when the lionesses were still around.

Just then, the zebra heard a far-off sound. He lifted his fine head and listened carefully, snuffling into the wind. There was no doubt about it, a vehicle was on its way, rumbling over the dusty track.

"Sorry, mate," said the zebra. "I've got to go. I can't be

seen sitting down here chatting with you. It's bad for my image, you see. Any minute now thirty tourists with cameras are going to come by, expecting to see a bit of wildlife, with the emphasis on "wild". I usually do peaceful grazing for them, but sometimes a bit of trotting goes down well. The ones with those video camera things like to see a bit of action."

And before the lion could say any more, the zebra dashed off through the grass, swishing his tail.

"I'm doomed," thought the lion, laying his great head on his paws. "No food means no lion. I won't see the end of the week."

He closed his eyes sadly. A minute later, an excited whisper interrupted his mournful thoughts.

"Look, Brenda, look! It's a lion. Isn't he majestic? Oh, I'm glad he's asleep. Quick, let me get a close-up. Oh, I'm just this close to being crushed by the jaws of a ravening beast!"

The lion opened one eye. Over a hundred yards away, three jeeps full of tourists had stopped. The speaker was a woman in khaki shorts and an odd hat. He raised his head to take another look

at her. The shorts showed all too clearly
that she was plump, and plump
means tasty. He looked at the
distance between them. It
was no good. The jeep
could go faster than
him any day.
Another perfectly
good meal would
go flying past.
The lion lay
down again
and yawned.

"Oh, Brenda, look at those teeth!
He's so fierce! Oh, I hope he'll do it
again. I didn't catch it that time. I must
have a photo of *teeth*!"

But the lion was asleep. He woke a
couple of hours later to hear chomping
close by. It was the zebra, looking very
pleased with himself.

"Hello, mate," said the zebra with a wink. "What did you get?"

"Get?"

"Yes, get, from the tourists, or the driver, you know."

"I didn't get anything," said the lion. "What did you think I would get?"

"Well, I usually get these crunchy thngs," said the zebra. "I think they're meant for horses, really, but they don't taste bad. Better than grass, anyway."

"But why do they give you crunchy things?" asked the lion.

"Well, it was the driver's idea," replied the striped animal. "He brought tourists out a couple of times and they didn't see a thing. It was afternoon, see, when most of us are sleeping. The tourists complained and asked for their money back, so he came out here and had a word with us. We promise to turn up and do typical animal-type things, and he brings us treats."

"But … but … I could…" The lion was beginning to get the glimmer of an idea (it just shows what practice can do). "I mean, couldn't I get some *food* that way?" he asked.

"Of course you could," laughed the zebra, "but you'd have to buck your ideas up, my lad. No more lazing around and yawning. They want prowling. They want pouncing. They want ravening and raging. If at all possible, they want roaring. They *don't* want you to look like a pussy cat."

"But I could do that!" cried the lion. "I could do prowling. I could put in a bit of practice on the pouncing. I could even raven and rage, though it might be a bit tiring. And I haven't roared in years, but I could give it a go."

"That's the spirit," grinned the zebra. "You'll be the star of the show! Look! You could do a bit now! Here they come back again!"

The lion gave it everything he had. He roared. He raged. He prowled and pounced. He swiped at imaginary tourists with his great paws and made sure the sun glinted on his claws. Then, as a grand finale, he wrapped his arms round the zebra's neck and swayed from side to side.

"Make it look good!" he hissed to the zebra, who had started to shake. "It's just an act, you know!"

Once he got into the spirit of the thing, the zebra was even more convincing. He neighed desperately. He staggered and curled his lips. In the end, he dropped to the ground and waved pathetically with one leg.

"They've gone," he whispered into the lion's mane. "The drivers don't like them to see the really gory bits."

"Let's just hope it worked," sighed the lion. The mock battle had taken up all his remaining strength.

He needn't have worried. Later that night, the driver of one of the jeeps came back to where the lion was resting.

"I brought a bit of dinner for you," he said. "You put on a great show, but we need you to be a bit beefier. No one likes a thin lion."

The lion tucked in with such gusto he forgot his table manners completely.

"So it's like that," said the driver. "Well, don't you worry, old chap. You put on a perfomance like today's twice a week and I'll keep you in dinners for the rest of your days. There's no need for you to overdo the roaring though. Just one or two will be more effective. Oh, and do a bit of mane-shaking as well, please. That always goes down well. It's great to have a lion on the trip again

We used to have some lionesses who were great, but they haven't been around recently. No idea what happened to them, I suppose?"

The lion had quite a good idea, but he shook his head. After all, why share a perfectly good dinner when you can have it all to yourself?

The
Talkative
Tree

Far away and long ago, a talkative tree caused incredible trouble. This is how it happened.

Not everyone realizes that trees talk, although you have probably heard them do it. The language is made up of rustles and creaks, swooshes and swishes. It is a language that only other trees understand. Of course, as young trees they can only understand trees from the same area. It takes a long time for an oak tree, say, to learn how to talk to a Japanese cherry, and some trees are too snooty to try to get on with their neighbours.

That wasn't the problem with the tree in this story. He was very friendly. Igthorp, as he was called, grew up as a young sapling in the middle of a big forest on a hill. All around him were trees of every kind. He loved to chat to the holly on his left and the maple on his right.

In fact, Igthorp liked to chat a little too much. No, the truth must be told. He liked to chat a lot too much. All day and all night he prattled away, and the other trees longed for a little peace and quiet.

It wasn't as if Igthorp said anything interesting. He simply came out with the first thing that came into his head. And he wasn't a very clever tree either, so what he had to say wasn't earth-shattering in any way. He talked about the weather—a lot. He wondered about what the sky was made of—a lot. He complained that worms were tickling his roots—a lot. He talked about his childhood, his bark trouble (don't ask—it was some kind of disease) and his awkward branch that was making him lean slightly forward.

Now, compared with you and me, trees are patient creatures. They can set about doing something and not mind if it takes a hundred years. The trees around Igthorp voted with their roots. Day by day, they edged a fraction of an inch away from their noisy neighbour.

Igthorp was too busy talking to notice it happening. After all, he never stopped for a moment to hear what anyone else said. But all the same, he felt a bit lonely the day he discovered he was totally alone. What happened was that a rabbit, eager to make a new home for her little ones, began digging among his roots.

That made Igthorp pause for a moment in what he was saying (and had been saying for the last seventy years) and look down. As he did so, he noticed for the very first time that he was standing on the top of a hill, completely alone. Down in the valley, on every side, there were trees as far as the eye could see. But he was alone. All the other trees had shuffled off and left him.

From far, far away he could hear a tantalizing whispering, as the other trees chatted to each other. But they were much too far to hear. Igthorp wiggled his roots to discourage the rabbit and started to talk. It was the only thing he knew how to do, and the fact that there was no one to hear him didn't change the fact that he had things to say.

"Ho hum," said Igthorp. "It looks like rain. Hmm. It looked like rain the day before yesterday, too. Hmm. I wonder if it will rain tomorrow. I wonder if it will really rain today. Hmm. That rabbit has gone. Good. Hmm. And my bark isn't quite so itchy today. Hmm. It was pretty itchy yesterday. It might be itchy again tomorrow. Hmm. That sky is getting greyer. It might be snow, not rain. Snow. That's a nice word. Sno-o-o-w. It's soft, like snow. Sno-o-o-w. Hmm. No, I think

I was wrong. It is going to be rain. Sno-o-o-ow. It's a nice word. Sno-o-o-w. But I think it will be rain. Hmm. I'm glad that rabbit's gone. Hmm. I'm glad my bark isn't itchy today. Hmm. Yes, I think it is going to rain. Today. Hmm."

You'll understand now why an entire forest, subjected to twenty-four hours of this every day, shuffled down the hill. Igthorp, however, was blissfully unware that he was impossible to live with. He had never stopped talking long enough for somebody to be able to tell him. As the clouds grew darker and darker, he muttered on.

Igthorp was right. It did rain. It poured down, drenching the tree and

everything around. The rabbit, out on the open hillside, scurried back among the big tree's roots, and Igthorp didn't have the heart to wiggle her out again.

The rain lashed down on Igthorp's leaves. The sky grew darker and darker. Almost overhead, a mighty roll of thunder drummed among the dark grey clouds. Then, suddenly, a flash of lightning streaked across the sky, looking for somewhere to strike. And what was the highest thing for miles around? It was Igthorp, still muttering to himself about the rain.

Strr-i-i-i-i-ke! The lightning sizzled on to Igthorp's topmost branches. For a moment he stood there, lit up and glowing. Then little tongues of flame licked among his leaves, leaving him looking blackened and dead.

There was a dreadful silence on top of the hill … until a very familiar voice struck up once more…

"Well, well, what was that? I've been sizzled! I've been struck! I knew it would rain. But I didn't know there would be lightning, too. How exciting! Sizzled and struck! Hmm. I wonder if it will rain tomorrow? I wonder if it will thunder tomorrow? I wonder if the lightning will come? They say lightning never strikes twice in the same place, but you never know. I might be lucky again. Hmm.

What's that wiggling? Oh, that rabbit again. Her ears look a bit singed. Serves her right. Hmm. It might be sunny in a minute. Is that a rainbow? I like rainbows. I wonder if it will rain tomorrow."

To anyone looking at him, Igthorp seemed a pitiful wreck. His leaves were dead. His branches were blackened and broken. His trunk was dark and charred. But inside, Igthorp felt just the same. He was ready for another seventy years of standing on the hill.

But Igthorp didn't have even seventy days there. At the end of the week, a tractor chugged up the tree with two men on board. They jumped off and took a long look at the tree.

"This one's dead," said the first man. "But it's pretty old. The wood should be fine inside."

They didn't even bother to chop Igthorp down. They looped a chain around his trunk and attached it to the back of the tractor. Then they drove off down the hill.

Igthorp felt a heaving in his roots. He heard a great screeching sound and began to topple towards the ground. With his mighty roots wiggling up into the air, it was difficult to tell which way up he was. A rather alarmed rabbit jumped down from the roots and hopped safely to the ground. She had noticed that the hole left by Igthorp might make the beginnings of a very fine home indeed.

Igthorp was dragged down the hill and along a rough track. And all the time he was talking. Of course, the men on the tractor just heard branches scraping on the ground and twigs breaking, but what Igthorp was really saying went something like this...

"Well, well, pulled up by my roots, well, well. Hmm. I wonder where they're taking me? I didn't realize my roots were so big. Where's that rabbit now? I can't go carrying rabbits around. Hmm. It doesn't seem to be here. That's good. Hmm. I wonder if it will rain tomorrow. Hmm. I wonder where we're going? I wonder if it's far? I wonder if we'll get there before the rain comes?"

It wasn't long before Igthorp found out. At the end of the track was a large building from which came a terrible noise. It was the sawmill. Happily chattering away, Igthorp was dragged towards the whizzing blades.

From that day, there was silence on top of the hill, broken only by the squeaking of tens, then hundreds, then thousands of baby rabbits, who popped up year after year. With so many wriggling, squiggling babies around, no more trees grew on top of the hill, and the whispering of the forest in the valley seemed very far away.

Meanwhile, the years passed and nothing was heard of old Igthorp. But a President had to be dragged from his office. "The table just wouldn't stop talking!" he cried, as the men in white coats took him away.

And a boy in Denmark refused to take his coat off because, he said, his chair told him it was going to rain.

This morning, I put my creaky old table out into the garden. I have bought a new one that looks much, much better. But, you know, it's a very strange thing. I'm sure that the hedge used to be nearer the house. And the tree by the pond no longer has its toes in the water. I expect I'm imagining it, don't you?

The
Supersonic
Sandwich

Some people are happy to play games and enter competitions just for the fun of it. "It's the taking part that counts," they cry, merrily shaking the hand of the winner. When tempers are frayed over the snakes and ladders board or sharp words are spoken on the tennis court, they beam and cry, "It's only a game!" To the kind of people who take games *seriously*, these puny players are intensely annoying.

Mrs. Brangs was a woman who took games seriously. She clenched her teeth in fury when her husband beat her at *Snap!*

She went purple with rage when Mrs. Wootten cheated at croquet. When Dora Devereaux's dog upset the Monopoly board in the middle of a tense battle between Mayfair and Marlborough Street, Mrs. Brangs almost lost the power of speech. She was a woman who liked to win—and to win by a wide margin.

Well, we've all met people like that. You may be one yourself. It may drive you wild when your friends giggle instead of concentrating during a dominoes duel. Perhaps you're the type who trains at dawn for sports day races and doesn't even consider the concept of second place. The difference with Mrs. Brangs (and I know you are not this kind of person, for you wouldn't have time to read this book if you were) was that she had a memory like an elephant. She remembered every point she lost to an opponent. She could recall the tiniest waiving of the rules and the slightest short-sightedness on the part of a referee. Stored up in her fevered brain was every game she had ever played and the conduct of her fellow players. She respected very few of them.

It is strange, really, that the people of Little Bassington didn't realize what seething emotions boiled beneath Mrs. Brangs' less-than-calm exterior. But then they were the relaxed kind of people I mentioned at the beginning. As they didn't take such things seriously themselves, it never entered their heads that an avenging angel lived in their midst. They thought dear Hilda was short on temper and long on determination, that was all.

But at 19, Alba Crescent, Mrs. Brangs was plotting her revenge. She wanted once and for all to show up her neighbours as the lily-livered, feeble-minded, shilly-shallying bunch of no-hopers she believed them to be. And fate played right into her hands.

One spring morning, young Doris Devereaux (and her dog) bounced into the village shop, where most of the older ladies of the village were buying their

weekly groceries and Mrs. Hilda Brangs was taking a peek at the answers in the back of last week's *Puzzler's Paradise* magazine to see if she had won anything.

"Oh, ladies!" gushed Doris. "It's *sooo* exciting!"

"What is?" asked several ladies, at once giving Doris the audience she was longing for. Mrs. Brangs sighed. She felt sure that nothing the silly woman could have to say could possibly be of interest to her. But she was wrong.

"The judges are coming!" cried Doris, her voice rising almost to a shriek in her excitement. "They're coming *here*! They're coming *next week*! It's too, too exciting for words!"

"Apparently not," muttered Mrs. Brangs under her breath, but even she had been interested by the mention of judges. It sounded as though some kind of deadly competition was afoot, and as we know, there is nothing Mrs. Brangs likes better than a contest of some description.

It took half an hour and two cups of tea for Doris to get her news out at last. It turned out that the judges of the *Biggest Ever Book of Records* were coming to the village to film a huge television spectacular. And whenever they did that, they liked local people to try to break some records.

Mrs. Brangs' brain was working overtime, but she spoke quite casually to the ladies in the shop.

"It'll mean bell-ringing," she said darkly, "for hours and hours and hours. I dread to think how long the world record is. It could be *weeks*!"

"No," said Doris triumphantly. "It won't be that. I can tell you definitely that it won't be that."

"How do you know? What else do you know? Has the list of competitions been published already?" Mrs. Brangs was desperate to know.

But Doris just giggled in a silly way. "There are workmen on the church tower," she said. "They won't be able to ring the bells for months."

Of course! Mrs. Brangs was furious with herself. She had known that all along and now she felt that she had revealed to the others just how interested she was in the whole project. Strolling as casually as she could (which frankly deceived nobody), she left the shop and dashed home. It was all she could do not to break into a run as she neared her gate.

As soon as she was indoors, Mrs. Brangs tore off her coat and hurried to the telephone. Her fingers literally shook as she dialled her nephew's number.

"Felix?" she cried, as soon as the ringing was answered. "Is that you?"

"Yes, of course," said a cross voice, similar in many ways to Mrs. Brangs' own.

"What do you want, Aunty?"

Mrs. Brangs explained at once. "I need you to look something up on your computer," she said. "It's about the *Biggest Ever Book of Records* coming to Little Bassington. I need to know what the competitions are going to be. Isn't there a spidersite or something you can check out? I need to know all there is to know about this, and I need to know by first thing tomorrow morning at the latest."

Felix hesitated. He felt that he was in a strong position for negotiating his next birthday present, and he was right. Two computer games and four CDs later, he had come to an agreement with his aunt.

Mrs. Brangs hardly slept. It was so hard to plan when she had no idea what the competitions would be. Next morning she was waiting inside the front door for the postman, almost gnawing the door

mat, when she heard his footsteps on the path. As the letters appeared, she seized them so forcefully that the postman felt in danger of losing his hand.

Back at her breakfast table, Mrs. Brangs discarded several bills and a brochure about stair-carpets and tore open Felix's envelope.

"Dear Aunty," she read, "here is the list you were looking for. I wouldn't attempt the trampolining if I were you."

Mrs. Brangs skimmed the list so quickly she couldn't take it in. Then she read more slowly, considering each item.

1. Shrimp-shelling: the number of shrimps that can be shelled in twelve minutes.

2. Trampolining: the number of back somersaults achieved in four minutes.

3. Pie-throwing: the number of pies to reach the target (details enclosed) in two minutes.

4. Leapfrog: largest team for a continuous game of leapfrog. Number to beat: 2,986.

5. Orange-juggling: highest number of oranges that can be kept in the air in continuous motion for a period of seven minutes (see rules for size and weight of oranges – no fruit substitutions allowed).

6. Marathon singing: longest period of non-stop singing. No repetitions (see rules for break times, decibel levels and measures of tunefulness).

7. Sandwich-making: highest
sandwich in two minutes using
standard bread and no two fillings
the same (see rules for buttering and
depth of filling allowed in each layer).
8. Ear-waggling: biggest range of
movement and longest sustained
waggling (no wiggling permitted)
using measures supplied.

For one mad moment, Mrs.
Brangs saw herself and the whole village
of Little Bassington leapfrogging madly
across the green. Then she pulled herself
together. There simply weren't 2,986 able-
bodied people in Little Bassington and she
didn't fancy the idea of leapfrogging with
strangers. Mrs. Brangs turned back to the
list to give it more serious consideration.

Shrimp-shelling? It wasn't a pleasant
thought. Mrs. Brangs had never enjoyed
seafood and as a result she had very little
experience of shelling shrimps. (It was

hard enough to say, never mind do.)
Besides, old Mrs. Moleworthy was a
fishmonger's daughter and had been
raised to do all kinds of barely speakable
things to fish. She was sure to win. Mrs.
Brangs discarded the shrimp-shelling with
some relief.

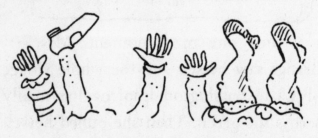

Trampolining? To be frank, Felix
might have a point in warning her away
from this one. Mrs. Brangs still felt full of
vim and vigour, but even she would have
to confess that she was not in her first
youth. Even with training, she was
unlikely to triumph over the slim girls
from the village school. No, trampolining
was out.

Pie-throwing was next on the list, and here Mrs. Brangs felt more confident. She had a powerful right arm and her left was not weak either. She imagined—oh, how vividly—throwing pies at the faces of all her enemies in Little Bassington (a large figure, though not as large as 2,986). But a quick look at the rules revealed that the target was to be a cardboard one, hung frighteningly high from a kind of scaffold. Some of the excitement of the event seemed to evaporate for Mrs. Brangs. She remembered, too, that the local policeman, Officer Pingling, had an even stronger right arm than her own. Would he feel it beneath his dignity to compete? If his recent pin-the-tail-on-the-donkey performance was anything to go by, almost certainly not. Mrs. Brangs still smarted from his scathing comments on her tail-positioning, during which he had given her more detail about a donkey's anatomy than she had felt was entirely essential. Maybe pie-throwing wasn't such a good idea.

The next two were easily disposed of. Leapfrogging was out of the question and juggling had never been Mrs. Brangs' favourite pastime. She could manage a fairly respectable three-orange performance, but anything more was beyond her, and she only had a week to practise. No, not orange-juggling.

Marathon singing? Now, that was more like it. Mrs. Brangs, it will not, I'm sure, surprise you to learn, possessed a powerful vocal instrument. In church on Sundays she belted out the hymns with no thought for the ear-drums of the members of the congregation in front of her. But was endurance really her greatest skill? To be truthful, Mrs. Brangs was stronger on volume than she was on the long haul.

And that bit about tunefulness in the rules could pose a challenge. Although Mrs. Brangs was personally quite confident of her pitch, she had overheard one or two comments that made her doubt the hearing of some listeners. Who could say what the judges would feel about her intonation? Mrs. Brangs mentally put marathon singing to one side. It was a possibility if nothing else appealed.

Running her eyes down the list, Mrs. Brangs saw that she had only two more to choose from – and one of those was ear-waggling. She knew that she need waste no time over that particular skill. She didn't have it, and that was that.

Only one more contest remained. Sandwich-making. As she read the rules in some detail, Mrs. Brang felt her interest rising. Surely this was absolutely the kind of thing at which she could excel? It called for speed and determination. Fine. It required planning and inventiveness. Also fine. And it was sure to involve a head-to-head, no-holds-barred play-off against Dora Devereaux, who prided herself on her culinary skills. Better than fine. This was truly *excellent*! Mrs. Brangs rubbed her hands and set about making her own list. Already, a sandwich of truly gigantic proportions was growing in her mind. Dora Devereaux didn't stand a chance.

Mrs. Brangs made her preparations with care. She had practice sessions in her own kitchen until her husband prayed he would never see another sandwich. She added and added and added to her list of fillings, discarding those that were fiddly or unreliable from a stackability point of view. She thought carefully about how she would set out her containers of fillings and buckets of butter. She even practised climbing up and down stepladders at speed—she was very confident, as you can see, that her own sandwich would tower over whatever the competition could do.

On the day of the contest itself, Mrs. Brangs was up well before the break of dawn, ready to make her final preparations.

Absolutely key to these was getting the butter to just the right degree of softness, so that it would spread easily but not fall off her knife. Mr. Brangs  was given the task of testing but his wife still hovered over him. At mistake at this stage could be critical.

At two o'clock, the village green was throbbing with people. The television crew had erected platforms from which the contests could be viewed. Areas were taped off so that the spectators could be kept at a distance. At ten past two precisely, the shrimp-shelling got off to a shaky start when Mrs. Moleworthy had one of her turns and had to sit down. Mr. Prentice, her chief opponent, objected that this gave her an unfair advantage. A

close and lengthy scrutiny of the rules revealed that competitors could shell shrimps on their heads if they wanted, and the contest got underway at last thirty-three minutes late. It was close, but Mrs. Moleworthy won by three shrimps, although she did not break the record in the *Biggest Ever Book of Records*.

The trampolining went off without a hitch, although one camera-man got too enthusiastic and was thumped in the ear by a bouncing elbow. The girls did well, but again, no world records were broken.

It was a different story in the pie-throwing, and Mrs. Brangs shuddered at how close she had come to almost total humiliation. Not only was Officer Pingling frighteningly good, but Mrs. Mabble from the school showed surprising form. It was later revealed that she had been national shot-put champion before her marriage but tended to keep it quiet because her husband thought it unladylike.

Mrs. Mabble walked off with the honours and a new world record. And Officer Pingling, dripping with sweat, stumbled home to the derisive cheers of several small boys who had met with his disapproval in the past.

The leapfrog, as Mrs. Brangs had suspected, was rather a disappointment.

Most of the leapers were very much less than froglike. The event ended in an ungainly heap with Mrs. Brang's husband somewhere at the bottom of it. But the director rubbed his hands with glee and said that it made good television.

Ear-waggling, it seemed, did not make good television. Apart from the fact that there was only one contestant (young Jimmy Barnes having been disqualified on the discovery of a contraption made of string and chewing gum attached to his left lobe), the waggling was so minor that the director shook his head. Mr. Devereaux (Dora's husband's ancient father) was given a consolation prize and hurried off the stage.

By now, it was late afternoon. Things were not running to schedule and a note of desperation had entered the director's voice. The light was fading. The camera-men were fading. And many of the spectators were fading, too. It was decided to hold the orange-juggling and the sandwich-making at the same time.

Mrs. Brangs, of course, protested. She objected that it would be off-putting to see oranges flying about out of the corner of her eye, but she had no support from Dora Devereux, who was always anxious to please. As a result, Mrs. Brangs was over-ruled and the contestants were told to prepare for the whistle.

Ready! Set! Wheeeeeeeeeeeeeee! The ladies roared into action. Bread was slapped on to tables. Butter flew from glinting knives. The first fillings splodged into place. After the first thirty seconds of panic, Mrs. Brangs hit her stride. She whistled through ham, corned beef, tuna and tomato, cucumber, pastrami, chicken mayonnaise and chopped egg with capers.

The sandwich was already up to her eyebrows, so she called for the stepladder and plunged on, knowing that she could not spare the time to look over her shoulder at what Dora Devereaux was doing behind her.

Avocado, jelly, bacon, salad, peanut butter, banana,

cheese, chocolate and honey
followed rapidly. Mrs. Brangs
steadied her tottering pile
with a firm hand.

"Just one minute left!"
called the official referee, and
Mrs. Brangs got her second
wind. Liver, duck, beef, lamb,
aubergine, peas, pork, oyster,
shrimp (despite her feelings
about seafood), cod, salmon,
trout, onion, turkey, sausage,
marmalade and marshmallow
were hurled between slices.
Mrs. Brangs was getting to
the end of her containers of
fillings. Only the stranger
ones were left. Ostrich, ice
cream, kangaroo, cauliflower,
squid and mango were
slapped into place. Panting,

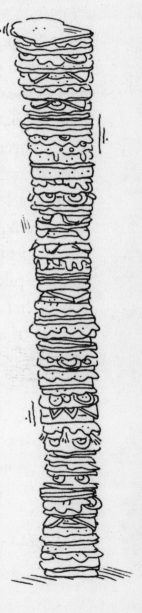

Mrs. Brangs glanced at the clock. Four seconds to go and no more fillings! In the heat of the competition she had been faster than she had ever managed in practice.

Three and a half seconds to go and Mrs. Brangs made the mistake of looking over her left shoulder. There was Dora Devereaux, wobbling dangerously at the very top of her stepladder and just about to place pilchards and peppers on the very top of her extraordinary sandwich. Mrs. Brangs tried to estimate the height of the two piles. It was impossible. But it was close. It was much, much too close for comfort.

Mrs. Brangs was bursting with the need to win. Just at that moment an orange shot up near her left ear. She had totally forgotten about the other contest, still going on right next door. In a moment of madness, Mrs. Brangs, beside herself with anxiety, stretched out her hand and caught an orange. She threw herself down the ladder, scarcely touching a step. *Chop, chop, chop! Slap, slip, slop!* Mrs. Brangs made short work of the orange and buttered another slice. Then she hurtled up the steps again, purple in the face, and plonked it on to the top of her pile, *just* as the final whistle sounded.

Neither Mrs. Brangs (who was now an unbecoming shade of puce) nor Dora Devereaux (collapsed under her table) heard much of the judging that followed.

Tape measures were produced, careful judgements as to depths of fillings were discussed, and each layer was examined minutely for traces of non-edible fillings or failure to butter. It seemed endless. By the time it was over, both ladies were fully recovered and gnawing their nails.

The announcer spoke to camera. "And what an exciting finish this has been. Once again *The Biggest Ever Book of Records* has brought you excitement and drama. And I can tell you now that the world record *has* been broken (wild cheers from the crowd) and that the effort of both ladies was truly outstanding (even wilder cheers from the crowd, a smile from Dora Devereaux and a weak wave from Mrs. Hilda Brangs)."

There was a dramatic pause. Then the announcer gave a wink and went on, "The highest sandwich, a quite staggering fifteen centimetres higher than the world record, was that of Mrs. Hilda Brangs! Congratulations, Mrs. Brangs!"

Mrs. Brangs' large bosom filled with pride. She was a champion. A world champion! And Dora Devereaux—*hah!*— was nowhere. Mrs. Brangs couldn't resist turning to look at her opponent, and what she saw sent a chill down her spine. There was Dora, standing next to the announcer. And Dora *had a sinister smile on her face.*

With a sickening certainty, Mrs. Brangs knew what the announcer was going to say before the wretched man opened his mouth.

"But there was, as I said, drama right up to the last moment. Sadly, Mrs. Brangs has been disqualified—*for deliberately disrupting another contest*! Let's see that replay now!"

Mrs. Brangs didn't need to see in slow motion the moment when her hand stretched out and caught the orange. She didn't need to see the pitiful face of the juggler as his hand closed around thin air and he dropped the lot as a result. Instead, she silently and stealthily crept away, vowing never to compete again ... but to devote all her energies to the dark and dreadful downfall of Dora Devereaux.

Mrs. Wolf's Problem

Mrs. Wolf had a problem and it can be stated right away. She had a son called William who was neither big nor bad. That, for a storybook wolf, is a truly terrible disgrace. Any wolf worth his or her salt has a long history of eating little pigs (preferably three at a time) and old ladies (especially when they're ill in bed). They are also supposed to frighten little girls, lurk about in the dark near flocks of sheep, and howl convincingly whenever there is a moonlit night.

William did none of these things. At first his mother thought that it was simply because he was a rather small cub and he would grow out of it. But even when he was fully grown, he only came up to her shoulder. His teeth, although sharp and white, were not big enough to inspire terror in most sensible people. His eyes, although bright and cunning, did not glint in a menacing way. He didn't drool. He didn't lurk. And his howl was rather tuneful and not at all heart-stopping.

Mrs. Wolf was in despair. First of all she tried sending him for lessons to old Septimus Wolf in the Deep Dark Forest. Septimus had a truly nasty reputation. A reputation that any wolf would be proud of. It was said that his lair was decorated with the bones of his victims. Others said that wasn't true. Septimus had eaten them, bones and all.

It was a rather cautious William who poked his snout into the old wolf's lair for his first lesson in viciousness.

Septimus, however, was asleep in front of a cosy fire. William expected him to leap up and start snarling at any moment, but instead a gentle snoring came from his slobbery lips. It was warm and comfortable by the fire, so after a while, William too lay down and went to sleep with his head on his paws.

When William woke up several hours later, it was already getting dark and time to go home again. Septimus, too, stirred and yawned.

"You must be young William," he mumbled. "Is it time for your lesson?"

William shook his head.

"No, it's time I was going home again. Shall I come back tomorrow?"

"That's a good idea," said Septimus, thinking of the generous fee he was going to receive from William's mother. "Little and often is the best way of learning."

That night, Mrs. Wolf questioned her son on what he had learnt that day.

"Was there any discussion of the importance of pouncing?" she asked. "Did you practise whining and scrabbling? Show me what you did."

William paused. "I don't think I should," he said truthfully. He knew that his mother was expecting great things of him and of old Septimus.

Mrs. Wolf nodded wisely. "Least said, soonest mended," she said. "I think I understand. I don't blame Septimus for swearing you to secrecy. A wolf's most vicious techniques are something he treasures. Come and have your supper. I'm sure you've deserved it."

For three weeks, William spent every day asleep in front of the fire with Septimus. It made him rather wakeful at night, so that he took to sloping off into the dark and sniffing around the sheep-pens and henhouses. Mrs. Wolf took this as a very good sign.

"Aah, the bloodlust is rising in him," she chortled, rubbing her paws together. "I knew his wolfishness would come out sooner or later."

Towards the end of the three weeks, the weather grew a little warmer, and one day when William trotted through the

trees to Septimus' lair, he found that there
was no cosy fire waiting.

"Hello, young William," said the
old wolf. "I think winter is over, and I'm
feeling a little peckish. Let's go and get
some breakfast."

Together, the master and the pupil
crept down the hill towards the meadow
where the new lambs were peacefully
grazing. The shepherd boy was chatting to
a girl at the bottom of the slope. Thirty
plump and pretty lambs grazed sweetly
on the green pasture.

"How innocent they look," said Septimus with satisfaction. "Off you go, my boy."

"Go where?" asked William. "I thought we were going to have breakfast together this morning."

"We are! What a sense of humour you have!" chuckled Septimus. "You're going to get it."

"Oh, fine. Where is it?" asked the young wolf, feeling peckish himself now.

"Why there!" Septimus' voice had taken on a sharper note. "The lambs. Look! I should think two each would do to start with. You can always go back for more if we're still hungry."

William was appalled, and he didn't hesitate to say so.

"What? You want me to hurt those dear little woolly things? I couldn't possibly do that. Surely it isn't necessary. I always get my breakfast from my mother. We could go and ask her for some."

Septimus began to look a little more like his reputation. The hair on the back of his neck rose up and his lip curled.

"Where," he snarled, "do you think your mother gets your breakfast from? What did you have this morning?"

"Lamb chops and a couple of eggs," said William promptly. "Ooooh! You don't mean...? She wouldn't...? Not my own dear mother?"

"She would. And she could. And she *did*!" growled Septimus. "And I see now why she sent you to me. Look, it's simple. All you have to do is sneak up to one of those lambs. Grab it round the neck. A quick bite and it's all over. Easy for the lamb. Even easier for you. Got the idea? Off you go!"

Well, William tried. Off he went, sneaking as well as he could (which was a bit loudly). Just as he got near to a plump little lamb, the creature looked up.

William froze. Then his instincts came into play. Not, unfortunately, his wolf-like instincts but his well-brought-up and polite instincts.

"Er ... excuse me," he said. "I'm looking for a spot of breakfast."

A look of alarm crossed the little lamb's face.

"I'm sorry," she said, "I don't think we've been introduced. My name is Lily Lamb. And you are...?"

"William Wolf!" cried the fearsome hunter. "Pleased to...."

But at the word "wolf", the lamb had taken to her heels, calling all her friends to come with her.

"Not," said Septimus drily, "a very promising start. How do you feel about chickens?"

"Delicious!" said William, smacking his lips.

"Then follow me, but be careful not to make any noise. The farmer here is an excellent shot."

"Really? What does he shoot?" asked William pleasantly, as he trotted along beside his teacher. He received in reply a look that would have made your blood run cold. It didn't make William's blood run even remotely chilly.

"Surely not!" he said. "I'm sure no one would be so nasty."

"Shhhh!" The wolves had reached the henhouse.

"There's a nice plump bird sitting just inside the door," hissed Septimus. "Lift up the latch with your nose, dive in, grab her, stop her squawking, and we're off. It's not much of a meal for two but, as you said earlier, you've already had your breakfast this morning."

"Right." William nodded. But he still wasn't sure. "Look, I wonder, is this really necessary?" he asked. "All that squawking, feathers in the mouth, claws in the nose, all that sort of thing. Just for a tiny bite of breakfast. Is it worth it?"

Septimus' reply was brief and to the point.

"Yes," he said.

"Well," WIlliam had a brilliant idea. "The thing is, as you can see, I'm new to this sort of thing, and I'm not completely sure about the correct fang position and that kind of detail. What about if, just this time, you show me? I'd be ever so grateful —and so would my mother, I'm sure."

"I'd ... er... love to oblige," said Septimus, "but the fact is, I'm not too keen on chicken really. I pretended to be, to encourage you. It's good stuff for a growing wolf. But I'd just as soon go without, myself. Perhaps we could call in on your mother after all. She might already have lunch on the table."

"Follow me!" called William, mightily relieved that he wasn't going to have to deal with feathers or feet.

Mrs. Wolf smiled broadly when the two wolves appeared at her door.

"Mr. Septimus," she cried, "this is an honour indeed. Please come in. What can I get you? A drink? A little snack? Just a bone to nibble on? I hope my boy has been behaving himself."

"I was thinking more along the lines of a four-course lunch," said Septimus. "We ... er ... we've been so busy this morning working on howling and lurking that we haven't had a moment to stop and get anything for ourselves."

William looked at Septimus. He knew perfectly well that no howling and no lurking had been done, unless you counted five minutes of whispering down by the henhouse. But Septimus gave him a big, special wink, that made William feel suddenly grown-up and proud.

"That's right," he said. "What have you got, mother? That howling is hard work. And as for lurking...."

"Of course it is," agreed Mrs. Wolf, bustling into action. "Just sit down over there, both of you. I've got some lamb, a couple of chickens, and two little piglets freshly caught this morning. I'm sorry there isn't a third, but security is getting very tight down at the piggery."

In no time at all, Septimus was falling upon the meal with undisguised relish. William looked down at his plate and felt a certain queasiness in his tummy. It was hard to feel quite the same about such things when he had seen lambs and chickens hopping about only an hour or so ago.

Once again, William said the first thing that came into his head.

"I'm thinking of becoming a ... what's the word for it? One of those creatures that don't eat meat. Oh, I know. A vegetarian!"

There was a shocked silence in Mrs. Wolf's house. When she spoke again, her voice had taken on an icier tone.

"Is this the kind of talk that you encourage in your pupils, Mr. Septimus

Wolf?" she asked. "Exactly how much benefit has my son been receiving from his lessons with you? William, answer me truthfully, how much killing have you done in the past three weeks?"

"K-k-k-killing?" William sounded appalled. "Why, mother, I wouldn't dream of doing anything like that. It would be cruel. Don't you agree, Mr. Septimus?"

The old wolf shot a look of appeal at his hostess.

"Dear lady, what can I say? I have *tried*. Goodness knows, I have *tried*."

"Really?" Mrs. Wolf's voice was chilling. "So, tell me William, how many creatures have you seen Mr. Septimus Wolf kill in the last three weeks?"

"Oh, mother, I can assure you, Mr. Septimus doesn't do anything like that either," said William eagerly. "Why, he doesn't even like chickens very much."

"That *does* surprise me," replied his mother, eyeing the old wolf's empty plate. "I would have said he liked them very much. Now, Mrs. Septimus, I think that you and I have a small matter of the refund of fees to discuss."

"Dear lady," Septimus shook his head regretfully. "When a pupil is simply not able to carry out the simplest task, it cannot be said to be the teacher's fault. A refund is out of the question, I'm afraid."

"Then I shall have to have a word with the Chairman of the Wolf of the Year Award," said Mrs. Wolf. "I believe it is to be presented next week, but you would know about that better than me, I think."

"This is blackmail!" quavered the old wolf. "Twenty years of ravaging and raging, and this is the thanks I get. So what if a wolf wants to take it easy in his old age? Have a heart, Mrs.Wolf!"

"Your mother," stated William's mother, "ravaged and raged until the day she died. And I begin to think that she's the only one in your family who did, Mr. Septimus. There has always been a lot of talk about you, but now I come to think of it, there's very little evidence that you were ever the fine, fang-sinking wolf you claim. You're a fraud, sir! I'll thank you to leave my table at once!"

William politely showed the visitor to the door. Outside, the old wolf paused.

"Here's a useful piece of advice, my boy. Leave it to the ladies. All that ravaging and ravening—they're much better at it than we are. You stick to a little lurking and a lot of good publicity and you'll be fine, just like me."

The other day, I heard of a truly nasty wolf over by the big hill. He goes by the name of William. The stories his mother tells of him would make your brains curdle. She doesn't believe a word of them, of course, but everyone else does, so she's as pleased as punch with her famous son. She says you learn a lot of useful things, listening through keyholes.

The Tiny Turnip

One day, Meryl's grandfather came to stay. He had recently retired from his job and was finding time hanging a little heavily on his hands. Meryl loved her grandfather, but he wasn't a very exciting person. He had been a bank manager, and although his eyes glowed when he talked about balances and borrowings, it wasn't the kind of thing that interested Meryl very much.

Meryl's mother tried to explain why Meryl didn't really want to spend too much time with him.

"The thing is, Dad," she said as gently as she could, "most eight-year-olds don't really care about pensions. That was why she ran out to play just now, not because she doesn't like you or anything."

The older man looked eager. "But, Dora, they should, you know! Why, if everyone gave a little thought to their future at Meryl's age...."

But his daughter cut him off.

"No, Dad. Tell me honestly, were you interested in banking when you were eight? I know it was a long time ago," she added mischievously.

Her father looked serious. He remembered a little boy with mud up to his knees, helping his own grandfather in the vegetable plot. He could almost smell

the earthy odour of the soil as it ran through his fingers. He could see the strong green shoots of the beans as they climbed up their poles. He recalled the sparkling drops of water you could shake from the leaves after a light shower of rain.

"No," he said. "I wasn't in the least bit interested in banking until I was over twenty. But I was lucky, you know. I ended up working in a field that I found fascinating. And it took up all my energy for forty years. The fact is, I don't know anything about anything else. I suppose I should try to develop some hobbies."

"How about making one of them something that a little girl of eight would enjoy?" suggested Meryl's mother. "She would love to share something with you."

That evening, Meryl's grandfather read her a bedtime story.

"You choose," said Meryl, and she tried not to show her disappointment when her grandfather picked out one of the books she had enjoyed when she was much younger. It was the story of the enormous turnip. You remember—a man grows such an enormous turnip that he can't pull it up, and it takes his wife and a cow and a pig and a cat and a dog and goodness knows how many other helpers to get the huge vegetable out of the ground.

In fact, Meryl's grandfather read it rather well, putting in funny voices and sound effects, so that Meryl actually found herself enjoying it.

"I don't think I've ever eaten a turnip," she said sleepily, when the story was over.

"What never?" cried her grandfather. "We must fix that tomorrow."

The next day, Grandfather set off for town with Meryl beside him in the car. "It's not really the right time of year," he said, "but you can buy anything anytime these days, so we should be able to find turnips somewhere."

But the strange thing was, there didn't seem to be a turnip to be had in the whole

place. They found parsnips and suedes and hundreds of carrots, but no turnips at all. Not even frozen ones.

"Never mind," said Meryl. "It doesn't matter."

But her grandfather was not happy. On the way home, he stopped at every farm shop and village store. No turnips. Back at home, he complained to Meryl's mother about the nearby shops.

Meryl's mother frowned. "Dad, this is ridiculous. First of all you couldn't talk about anything but pensions and profits. Now you're obsessed by turnips. Are you feeling well? Maybe you need to get away somewhere."

"I am away somewhere, remember," said her father. "Perhaps it's time I went home, if I can't talk about anything that interests you. After all, I've got to face the future sooner or later. And I *do* have a decent pension!"

Although his daughter tried hard to persuade him to stay, Grandfather's mind was made up. He set off for home the next morning, looking quite cheerful.

For two weeks, nothing was heard of him. Then, one morning, Meryl received a letter. Inside was a tiny packet and a card. It said, "Meryl Sarah Batten Maskovin, I challenge you to a champion turnip contest. The person having grown the largest turnip six months from today will be the winner. Your seeds are enclosed. Good luck!"

In the tiny packet, there were some even tinier seeds. Meryl hurried to find her mother.

"Hmm," said that lady, "so he hasn't forgotten about turnips."

She showed Meryl where to find her gardening books and helped her to dig over a patch of ground at the end of the garden. Then she left her to it.

Once a week, for the next few months, Grandfather telephoned to find out how things were going. When Meryl reported that she had sown her seeds, he said airily, "Oh yes, mine went in last week." When Meryl, with excitement, told him that tiny green shoots were appearing, he said, "Tiny? Oh." When she said that each shoot had two little leaves, he made a tut-tutting noise and sighed, "Only two? Really?" Each week, Meryl came away from the phone feeling depressed, and each week, her mother comforted her.

"I'm sure you are doing just as well as he is," she said, "and anyway, there's still a long way to go yet. He may not get as much sunshine or rain as us in the next few months. Don't worry."

But Grandfather's reports continued to be glowing as far as his own crop was concerned.

"Mine are looking great," he would say. "How about yours, Meryl?"

"Well, they're fine," Meryl would reply, "but I'm not really sure what they're supposed to look like."

Meryl weeded and watered. She thinned out lots of the weaker plants and protected the others from greedy birds and rabbits. Her next-door neighbour put his head over the fence and congratulated her.

"Those are the best-looking turnips I've seen in a long time," he said.

After that, Meryl felt more confident when she talked to her grandfather.

"Good, good," he said. "But are you talking to them?"

"Talking to what?" asked Meryl.

"Talking to the turnips," said her grandfather. "I talk to mine every day. And I play them music, too. It helps them to grow. Only classical, of course."

Meryl discussed the talking-to-plants issue with her mother.

"It can't do any harm, I suppose," was her verdict. "Meryl, does your grandfather sound … well … *odd* in any way on the phone?"

"No, he sounds better, really," said Meryl. "Sort of lively. And you know he hasn't mentioned pensions for weeks."

The final day of the challenge came at last. Meryl was up early, making sure her turnips looked their best. At half-past-eleven, a car drew up outside.

Meryl watched through the window as a man got out. She hardly recognized him! Instead of a dark suit, this man was wearing jeans and a sweater. His hair was longer and his face was tanned. He looked well and happy and he walked with a spring in his step, carrying a big bunch of flowers in his arms.

"Where's my favourite gardener?" he cried, hurrying up the front path.

"You look wonderful, Dad," smiled Meryl's mother, as she hugged him.

"These are for you," said her father. "All my own work. I've been doing quite a bit of gardening since I last saw you. As well as other things."

Meryl's mother frowned. "Don't let her be too disappointed, will you?" she whispered. "She has worked really hard, but I think those turnips are pretty average. Tell her she's done well, won't you?"

But Meryl was calling loudly from the back door.

"Hurry up! Come and see my turnips. They look great!"

And they certainly did!

"I know yours will be bigger," said Meryl, "but I'm still quite proud of mine. They're the first things I've ever grown by myself. And it was fun."

"You're a very clever girl, Meryl," smiled her grandfather. "It took me years and years and years to try something new. And you're right. It is fun. But as for my turnips, well, they certainly are absolutely extraordinary. I brought the biggest one along with me."

"Show me! Show me!" cried Meryl. "Is it in the car? Can I go and get it? Or will it be too big for me to carry?"

Meryl's grandfather grinned. "No," he said, "it isn't too big for you to carry. In

fact, it fitted right into my pocket here!"
And he fished out one of the tiniest turnips
you have ever seen!

Meryl and Meryl's mother and
Meryl's grandfather collapsed in laughter
on the path.

"I'm good at growing flowers,"
giggled her grandfather, "but turnips are
not my strong point. I'm afraid I slightly
misled you on the phone."

"I'd say you have quite a talent for fiction," said his daughter.

"Well, it's funny you should say that," replied Grandfather. "That is something else I've been doing. In fact, I've been quite successful. My first story for children is being published next year. It's called *The Tiny Turnip*.

That was some years ago now. Maybe you've read it?

Beep! Beep! BEEP!

Miss Evangeline Postle was a lady well advanced in years. She looked exactly what she was—which was a retired schoolteacher with a very small pension but very definite ideas on any subject you cared to mention.

Villagers were used to seeing Miss Postle riding to the Post Office on her ancient bicycle and arguing about the price of sausages with Mr. Bangs the butcher. Miss Postle was liberal in the use of her bell and not very tolerant of road use by other cyclists or pedestrians. On the subject of car drivers she was even more opinionated. To listen to her, you would think they were responsible for most of the problems of the world today.

In view of this, it was an enormous shock to Miss Postle's neighbours when the brightly decorated car of a driving school drew up outside her cottage one sunny day.

Miss Postle hopped in and gripped the wheel. Then with a great grinding of gears and screeching of brakes, she made her way by fits and starts down the main street, causing cyclists, pedestrians *and* car drivers to flee in all directions.

Quite quickly, the story went round the village that Miss Postle had come into a little money. An elderly aunt had died and left her a small inheritance. Miss Postle, it seemed, had decided there and then to buy herself a little car. There only remained the small matter of learning to drive.

That, as I say, is the story that went round the village, but some listeners shook their heads doubtfully.

"It's hard to believe that Miss Postle still has aunts alive," said Mr. Marvel at the garage. "Not that I wouldn't welcome the extra business if she does buy a car."

Mrs. Goodrich the minister's wife agreed. "I can't believe she has relatives older than herself," she said. "But has anyone actually asked Miss Postle? I'm quite sure she would tell the truth if we enquired."

However, no one wanted to be the person to ask Miss Postle. She could be very brisk in her replies, and after all, it was only curiosity that was prompting the question.

In the end, Mrs. Goodrich instructed Mr. Bangs the butcher to do the asking.

"After all," she said softly, with a meaningful smile, "your dealings with Miss Postle are already ... well ... lively, shall we say. Things can hardly get worse, can they? And there is nowhere else for her to buy her sausages around here. You must ask her tomorrow."

Mr. Bangs grinned. He wasn't at all afraid of Miss Postle. Next morning, when the schoolteacher came into his shop, he got straight to the point.

"Good morning, Miss Postle," he beamed. "The whole village is talking about your good luck. A nest egg from an elderly aunt, wasn't it?"

Miss Postle scarcely drew breath before she gave Mr. Bangs a substantial piece of her mind. She told him, first of all, that it was none of his business. She told him, second of all, that it was the rudest thing she had ever heard to ask a lady about her finances. Lastly, she said, she wouldn't dream of telling him if he was the last man on earth, and it wouldn't matter how hard he begged.

Mr. Bangs nodded calmly and went back to weighing the sausages. The other customers in the shop (and it was strangely busy this morning), drew breath and pursed their lips. Harsh words indeed!

In fact, Mrs. Goodrich was not the only person to go home with the feeling that Miss Postle's reaction was just a little bit extreme. Did she have something to hide?

Over the next few weeks, the sight of Miss Postle behind the wheel of the driving school car became very common. Very, very gradually, she stopped jerking down the road and started to drive more smoothly, although at an extraordinarily fast speed for a woman of such normally cautious habits.

"I don't know what's the matter with her," said Mr. Marvel. "My father went to school with Evangeline Postle and she was as straightlaced then as she is now. It's as if she becomes a different person behind the wheel of a car."

Mrs. Goodrich nodded. She found the whole thing very puzzling. Miss Postle was obviously keen to buy her car as soon as possible. She had a lesson every day and sometimes twice a day.

"It must be costing her a fortune," said the Post Mistress. "My youngest is learning at the moment, and he only has one lesson a week. It's all we can do to manage that. Miss Postle's legacy must have been a bit larger than we thought."

And Miss Postle certainly seemed to have undergone a change of character. She had never hesitated to tell people what she thought about things, but she had usually been polite (just about!) Now it was very different. Worst of all were her meetings with Mr. Bangs the butcher. Nowadays, crowds of people squeezed into the shop to hear their daily encounter. It was better than watching television.

"What," Miss Postle would enquire in icy tones, "do you call that?" She pointed her skinny finger at the counter.

"I call that a pork chop, Miss Postle," the butcher would reply. "And a very fine one it is, too."

"Fine? You pathetic poltroon! It looks as if it came from a piglet—and a puny one at that! How you have the barefaced effrontery to serve me something like that I can't imagine."

"Miss Postle, I could pretend to delve about under the counter and come up with another chop," said Mr. Bangs,

"but it would be a charade. You will not find a better chop than this in the whole country. As for the pig that supplied it, he was a noble animal of almost impossibly immense proportions. You malign the memory of a magnificent beast."

"It surprises me, Mr. Bangs, that you do any business at all if you always contradict your customers," retorted Miss Postle. "I will take that chop, but I expect to pay a pittance for it. It is certainly not worth more."

Talk of the bad blood between Miss Postle and the butcher went around the whole village in no time. By the time it got back to Mr. Marvel, there was talk of knives being brandished and threatening letters being pushed through letterboxes. None of this was true, of course, but

there was enough truth in it to make everyone believe it. Mr. Marvel repeated everything to Mrs. Goodrich. And Mrs. Goodrich nodded wisely.

"I feel that there is more to this than meets the eye," she said. "And I have half an idea that I know what it is, but even I don't quite believe what I'm thinking."

And more than that she would not say, even when Mr. Marvel attempted to bribe her with a free oil check and wheel washing.

Now Mr. Marvel's sister's son-in-law worked at the place where driving licences were issued. The day came when Mr. Marvel was able to announce to all his customers that Miss Postle had a driving test booked for the following week.

"She won't pass in a million years," he said. "She drives much too quickly and always beeps as she comes round that

sharp corner near the butcher's. You're not supposed to do that, but I don't suppose she listens to a word her instructor says."

But Mr. Marvel was wrong. On the following Thursday, Miss Postle pulled up outside her gate in a slinky silver sports car—and she was alone. Clearly, she had passed her test and bought a car on the same afternoon.

"It's not the kind of car I expected her to buy," said the Post Mistress. "It's rather, well, racy, don't you think?"

"I think," said Mrs. Goodrich, "that it's a little difficult to guess what to expect of Miss Postle these days, and I rather think there are more surprises to come."

The next morning, half the village jammed into the butcher's shop for Miss Postle's daily duel with Mr. Bangs. They hoped that he would ask about the car.

But the spectators were to be badly disappointed. Miss Postle did not come into the shop. She whizzed up to the door in the little sports car and leaned heavily on the horn. Surely she didn't now expect Mr. Bangs to serve her on the pavement?

But Mr. Bangs was behaving out of character as well. He took off his apron and put on his best jacket.

"I'm sorry, ladies and gentlemen," he said, "but I'm closing early today. The shop will open again in a week's time. You have all bought so much meat in the last few weeks that I'm sure your freezers are full. Goodbye!"

He walked out of the shop and, to the astonishment of everyone present, climbed into the passenger seat of Miss Postle's car. The little silver machine had

zoomed away before most of those
watching had closed their mouths.

"What?"

"Where?"

"Why?"

"But I don't understand!" wailed
the Post Mistress. "I thought they hated
each other!"

Only Mrs. Goodrich was looking
rather smug. "Didn't you ever notice how
much they enjoyed their rows?" she
asked. "I was suspicious from the start. I
always wondered what would happen
when Miss Postle met her match, and now
we know! I think they'll be very happy."

"Happy? What do you mean? Oh,
you don't mean...? You can't mean...?
Miss Postle and Mr. Bangs? No, no. That's
as unthinkable as..."

"As Miss Postle zooming around the village in a silver sports car?" asked Mrs. Goodrich mildly. "Knowing what a terrible village this is for gossip, Mr. Bangs and Miss Postle clearly decided to keep their relationship a secret. But it had to come out somewhere."

"But where have they gone?" cried the Post Mistress.

"I imagine they have gone on their honeymoon," smiled the minister's wife. "Probably somewhere a very long way from here."

"But," the Post Mistress decided to take a firm line (and she sounded, to tell you the truth, remarkably like the old Miss Postle), "they're not *married*!"

"Ah, now that's where I am at a slight advantage," said Mrs. Goodrich. "I happen to know that my husband is busy this morning."

It took several days for the news to sink in, and one comment above all the rest was heard from the villagers.

"We're going to miss those rows in the butcher's! It really was the highlight of our day!"

But they need not have worried. After all, Evangeline and Mr. Bangs had been enjoying rowing like an old married couple for months. Why should they want to stop now?

Biggles' Bubbles

ngela wanted a hamster. She begged and she pleaded. But her father was surprisingly firm.

"There will be nothing in my house," he said, "that looks anything like a rat. And that's final."

Angela pointed out that hamsters *were* nothing like rats. She waxed lyrical about their cute little noses and their bright beady eyes. When that didn't work either, she tried whining and moping. Her father was not impressed.

"I don't want whining and moping in my house either," he said. "But if I had to choose, I'd pick a whine and a mope over a hamster any day."

Angela said "Hmmmmph!" very loudly and stomped upstairs to think of another plan. She really, really wanted that hamster.

To make matters worse, Angela had already told her friends at school about the soon-to-arrive hamster. It was very embarrassing that it wasn't about to arrive, soon or otherwise.

Angela sat on her bed and thought hard. Then she sat on the floor and thought some more. Finally, she crawled under the bed and thought again. She found that different places sometimes worked better, but today nothing was working very well.

It was only when Angela finally crawled out and brushed the various bits of fluff and sweet-papers off her skirt that she did have one possible idea. She could buy a hamster from her savings and hide it. Her father didn't usually come into her room. He claimed he didn't want to catch something nasty. So how would he know if there was a hamster there?

At supper, Angela's father had a few more words to say on the subject of rats and their relatives.

"Don't," he said, "think that you can sneak a hamster-rat into this house without my knowing. I'll be able to *sense* the thing is here. And anyway, those little wheels they run round and round always squeak. Believe me, I'd *know*."

Angela chewed her chips in silence. It looked as if the hamster plan would have to be put to one side for the moment.

As she served up dollops of ice cream later, she started to work on Plan B.

"Da-a-a-ad," she said.

"Ye-e-e-es," said Dad.

"What if I had another kind of pet, instead of a hamster?"

"No puppies, no kittens, no rabbits, no gerbils, no jerboas, no chinchillas, no guinea pigs, no mice, and obviously, no rats," said her father. "What were you thinking of?"

Angela screwed up her face.

"So it's really nothing with fur?" she enquired.

"Nothing with fur, with beady little eyes, with twitchy little whiskers or nibbly little noses," said Dad. "They all give me the creeps."

Angela opened her mouth...

"And reptiles are out, too," said Dad. "No creepy-crawly slimy things."

Angela paused to make sure he had finished.

"So I could have anything apart from the nibbly, creepy, twitchy things?" she asked sweetly.

Dad looked suspicious. He ran rapidly through his ancient *Encyclopedia of Animals* in his mind. No, he'd covered everything

"Yes, any normal pet other than the ones listed above," he said warily.

"So I could have a fish, then?" asked Angela, "in a little tank?"

"Not a piranha or a baby shark or anything?" queried her parent.

"No, just a goldfish," said Angela. And her father agreed.

That is how Biggles the goldfish came into the house. He was a fat, orange fish who did nothing all day except swim around his tank and blow bubbles. Angela supplied him with a cunning little bridge he could swim under and some plastic weed he could swim through, but Biggles didn't seem very interested. He preferred to circle his tank in a serene way and blow bubbles. It was very peaceful to watch.

Angela was pleased with her new pet. He was much less demanding than a hamster and he didn't keep her awake at

night running around on a little wheel.
She decided her father had been right
about some things after all. But after a
couple of weeks, Angela began to worry.
Her bedroom was on the sunniest side of
the house, and wherever she positioned
Biggles' tank, the water always seemed to
get quite warm. She didn't think this was
good for him, and after an hour in the
library looking at goldfish books she was
sure it wasn't good for him.

"Da-a-a-ad," said Angela at supper
that evening.

"Ye-e-e-es?"

"I think Biggles would be much better down here, where it isn't quite so sunny. Could you help me bring his tank down tonight?"

Much to her surprise, her father agreed at once. "I'd hate you to wake up to boiled fish one morning," he said, showing a rather unpleasant imagination, Angela thought.

So Biggles came downstairs and now swam majestically around in the middle of the living room. Angela's father took to watching him as he swooshed round and round.

"It's very soothing after a day in the office," he told Angela. "And it's a good deal more entertaining than most of what's on the television these days."

One evening, when Angela was at her dancing class, her dad sat in front of

Biggles' tank for a long time. Sometimes he talked to the little fish, and sometimes he was silent. But he felt very rested and peaceful. Until...

"Get up, you fool! It's time to pick up Angela!" came into his brain. Angela's father shook his head. No one had said a word, but it was almost as if Biggles had put the thoughts into his mind. He stared hard at the little fish, and the words, "I did!" came into his head. Angela's dad grabbed his coat and set off to pick up his daughter, but he felt pretty worried about what had just happened. Had he spent too many evenings staring at a fish tank? Was he going quietly mad?

Angela and her father didn't usually have heart-to-hearts, but that evening in the car, her dad found himself telling her all about the message from Biggles.

"I know this sounds ridiculous, but you don't think it could be telepathy, do you?" he asked her.

"Well, it's never happened to me," said Angela, feeling that if anyone should get secret messages from Biggles it was her —he was her fish after all.

When they got home, father and daughter sat on either side of the fish tank and gazed at Biggles.

"The fact is, you've got me a bit worried, my lad," said Dad.

"I'm not a lad," said Biggles, straight into Dad's head.

"There! Did you hear that?" Angela watched in astonishment as her father jumped up and down on the chair and pointed wildly at the tank.

"I didn't hear a thing," said Angela, "and I think you should get down from that chair or you'll break it."

But a look of illumination had crossed her father's face.

"I know what it is!" he cried. "I've got it! Now I know how those code-breakers in the war felt! I've really got it!"

"I think you've really got problems," said Angela, backing towards the door. Dad waved her back impatiently.

"No, look, it's Morse code! He's blowing bubbles in Morse code! Big bubbles for dashes and little ones for dots. My brain was understanding it, even though I wasn't."

Angela shook her head. He had lost his marbles completely. But Dad was pointing eagerly.

"Look! Look! He's saying, 'Nothe!' Nothe? That doesn't make sense. Nothe?"

"It does, you know," said Angela, feeling herself becoming interested. "It isn't 'nothe'. It's 'not he'. He's telling us he's a girl!"

Biggles did a loop-the-loop to show she was right.

Dad sat down on the carpet with a bump. Surely this wasn't happening.

Angela had more practical matters in mind.

"DO YOU WANT A NEW NAME?" she shouted at the glass.

Biggles began blowing bubbles at a furious pace.

"Wait!" cried Angela. "Dad! I need you to translate!"

"Don't they teach you anything at school?" grumbled Dad, but he started to concentrate on Biggles all the same.

"She says," he said slowly, "that you don't have to shout. She can lip read."

"Oh," Angela lowered her voice. "Biggles, would you like a new name?"

"No," said Biggles.

"Is there anything you need?" asked Angela.

Dad translated. "It's very boring in here. The bridge and the weed are not very exciting."

Angela could see that for a Morse-Code-using-goldfish, they might not be.

"What would you like?" she asked. "A plastic castle?"

"No!" (Even Angela could easily understand that now.)

"Some model lobsters or divers?"

"No! I was thinking more in terms of another fish. A boy fish."

"Just a minute," said Dad. "How old is this fish? I'm not sure I can allow mixed tanks under my roof. Goodness knows what would go on. We could be over-run with baby fish before we knew where we were. Ooops. Forget I said that, Angela!"

"Don't be daft, Dad," said Angela. "You'll have to talk to Biggles about that."

But Biggles was lying on the bottom of the tank and waving her fins in mock despair. She let it be known that she felt she was much too young to be settling down and having baby fish, and Angela's dad need have no worries on that score. But she really would like a friend. And if the man with the big mouth insisted, it could be a female fish, only, how was he going to tell?

Biggles was right. Neither Angela nor her father had the faintest idea how to tell a boy fish from a girl fish. They spent ages dithering in the pet shop. In the end, they simply bought the liveliest fish they could find.

Biggles was overjoyed. It was no longer peaceful to watch her swimming around her tank. She and her new friend dashed around all day, never still for a second. And the sad thing was that Biggles was now moving much too quickly for her bubbles to be understood.

It wasn't long before Angela's Dad began to feel embarrassed about the fact that he had once been able to talk to a fish. When Angela casually mentioned that she was going to write an essay about it for school, she suddenly found herself the proud owner of a hamster—and a very bad memory!

The
Very Tidy
House

My Aunt Martha likes everything to be clean and tidy. She doesn't seem to think of anything else. To tell you the truth, it's not very comfortable being at her house. If she gives you a glass of orange juice, she hovers over you as you drink it, ready to whisk it away before it can make rings on the polished furniture or spill on the spotless carpet.

I'm very glad to say that my mother is not like that at all. In fact, she's the opposite. All our furniture has rings on it, and our carpet has not been spotless for years. None of us remembers what colour it was to start with. Nowadays it's a kind of greyish brown.

The thing about my mother, though, is that she's *interesting*. She's the kind of person it's fun to know – and that is more than can be said for Aunt Martha. Mum says that life is too short for dusting.

She'd rather be learning new spells or practising for her Part VIII Magician's Certificate. Yes, she does magic, and we live in a house that is comfortable, even if it's not particularly clean.

I did ask Mum once if she couldn't say a spell to clean the place up, but she said that life was too short for that, as well. It's very hard to believe that she and Aunt Martha are sisters.

Aunt Martha isn't the sort of person you have long, cosy chats with, but one day I asked her why she didn't do magic as well.

Aunt Martha shuddered.

"Magic," she said, "is such *untidy* stuff. You can never be exactly sure how it will turn out. I like things to be neat and sensible. I've no time for that airy-fairy nonsense. Besides," she added, after a short pause, "I'm not very good at it."

Well, I do know what Aunt Martha means about magic being untidy. Mum can do brilliant things, but she also has the most dreadful disasters. Once, trying to make the flowers in her garden grow a bit more vigorously, she created a forest that four qualified tree-surgeons spent two weeks removing. Her attempts to paint the outside of the house without climbing a ladder were fairly disastrous, too. She had forgotten to leave the windows out of the spell, so they got painted as well.

I told Mum what Aunt Martha had said about tidiness that night at supper.

"Well, there you are," said Mum, laying down her spoon with emphasis (and splattering the cat in the process). "A little more untidiness is exactly what that woman *needs* in her life. We should try to help her."

A faraway look came into Mum's eyes, and she rested her elbow absent-mindedly in her soup as she thought. I knew what *that* meant.

"*Please*," I said, "please, please, *please*, don't put a spell on Aunt Martha. Remember what happened to the boy who delivers the newspapers when you tried to help *him*. Aunt Martha is happy as she is. Please leave her alone!"

Mum looked at me and lifted her elbow out of the soup.

"All right," she said. "I promise I won't interfere unless she asks for help. Then, of course, it would be unkind not to do what I can."

It didn't seem at all likely that Aunt Martha of the spotless carpets would ever ask for help from Mum of the spotted everything, so I was happy. As things turned out, that was very silly.

One day after Christmas, Aunt Martha was scraping snow away from her front path when she slipped. She didn't break anything, but the doctor said it was a bad sprain and she mustn't walk on it for a week.

"A week?" Aunt Martha was aghast. "How am I going to manage with all this to do?"

The doctor looked around at her spotless living room and shrugged his shoulders.

"It *is* only a week," he said.

But Aunt Martha started worrying straight away, and by the time Mum and I went to visit her that evening, she was in a terrible state.

"Mary," she said, "it's dreadful. I sit here and I can *feel* the dust settling. This house is getting dirtier by the second, and there's not a thing I can do about it!"

Mum didn't know what to say.

"It looks fine to me, Marthy," she said. "I think if I tried to do anything it would only get worse."

"No, no!" cried Aunt Martha in alarm. "I didn't mean that you should do anything. I know that housework isn't your ... isn't something you enjoy. It's just that I don't know how I can stand being here for a week with things getting worse and worse and worse."

"Why don't you come and stay with us?" I asked. "Then you won't have to look at it, and when you are better and can come home, you can sort it out really quickly, can't you?"

Aunt Martha looked doubtful. I could see she was weighing up in her mind the torture of seeing her perfect home growing less perfect and the even worse torture of seeing our already less-than-perfect home all day and every day. She shuddered and smiled politely.

"No, no, that's very kind," she said, "but I think I'll stay here. I wouldn't want to put you to any bother washing sheets and so on."

"Oh, you needn't worry about that," said Mum cheerfully. "The sheets you used last time are still on the spare bed. No trouble at all."

Aunt Martha's pale face lost even more colour.

"I'll be fine here," she said firmly.

But two days later, she was not fine. The almost invisible dust on her surfaces was too much for her. Convinced that a little light polishing would not do her any harm, Aunt Martha staggered around the furniture with her duster and can of polish. The result was another fall. This time she twisted her knee.

Now Aunt Martha had no choice. She *had* to come and stay with us (but she insisted on bringing her own sheets) and put up with our level of untidiness and messiness. I could see that she wasn't happy, but at least she wasn't tottering around about to do herself more harm. I think it was pretty clear to Aunt Martha from the start that it would take more than a duster and a tin of polish to make a difference in *our* house.

I was quite busy over the next few days, trying to entertain Aunt Martha. I brought her soothing drinks and books from the library. I read to her when she wanted to close her eyes (which was quite a lot of the time) and helped her up and down stairs as necessary. I didn't stop to wonder what Mum was doing. After all, she was spending quite a lot of time in the kitchen, making meals for the invalid.

At last the doctor pronounced Aunt Martha fit to go home. She moved a bit stiffly still, but I could see she was relieved that her exile was over. Mum and I drove her back and helped her into the house. It still looked spotless to me, but Aunt Martha began rolling her sleeves up right away. She disappeared into the kitchen to find cleaning things without even waiting to say goodbye.

"Cover me!" hissed Mum, in a very melodramatic whisper. Before I could stop her, she had slipped into the under-stairs cupboard where Aunt Martha kept her vacuum cleaner and ironing board.

"Mum! What are you doing?" I hissed in turn. "She's just coming back!"

Mum emerged from the cupboard just as Aunt Martha returned with a bucket of soapy water and an armful of cleaning things. She just glimpsed Mum shutting the cupboard door.

"Just checking the hinges," said Mum. "You can't be too careful." And she hurried me out of the house.

All the way home, I begged Mum to tell me what she had been doing in the cupboard.

"I was just trying to make things a little easier for my poor sister," said Mum. "You know, many vacuum cleaners are not very efficient. I just souped hers up a little. She'll hardly notice."

"Souped it up?" I asked faintly. "You mean by magic?" I had visions of Aunt Martha flying along behind a rocket-powered vacuum cleaner, zooming around her house at fantastic speed.

"Yes, of course by magic," said Mum. "I just made it more powerful. It will pick up a speck of dust at a hundred metres now."

A cold feeling crept up to my knees.

"If it will pick up a speck of dust from a hundred metres," I said quietly, "what will it pick up from one metre or even one centimetre?"

Mum looked reflective. She slowed down and put her head on one side.

"Well...," she said, "you may have a point there."

Before I could say another word, she had done a completely illegal U-turn in the middle of the road and was speeding back to Aunt Martha's house.

We could tell before we stopped the car that it was too late. Much too late. There were no curtains at Aunt Martha's windows. The front door was open.

Inside, a horrible scene met our eyes. There was no dust. There was no furniture. There were no carpets on the floors or lamphades on the lamps. The house was as empty as a house can be. And there was no sign of Aunt Martha. The only thing we could find was the vacuum cleaner, standing in the middle of her bedroom floor and burping gently.

I looked at Mum. I didn't have to say anything.

"Give me a moment," she said. "It will all be fine. I just need to think."

She sat down in the middle of the floor and thought, but I could see a look of panic in her eyes.

"I don't think I can get her back," she said. "Or the furniture. The only thing I can think of doing is to turn back time to a moment before this happened. It's the most difficult kind of magic of all to do.

But I don't have any option. We'll need to go home to get my books."

The next two hours were torture. I didn't know whether to have faith in Mum's magic or cry for Aunt Martha. It was like being in limbo. At last Mum emerged from her room with a smile on her face.

"I think I've got it," she said. "Let's get back there straight away."

"Do we have to go back?" I asked. "Aren't you turning time back here as well as there?"

"Yes," said Mum, "but I need to make sure I've got it right. I can't bear to think of my poor sister in that vacuum-cleaner bag. For one thing, she'll hate all the dust in there."

Back at Aunt Martha's house, everything was very quiet. Mum stood in the middle of the kitchen and told me to shut my eyes as she said the spell. It didn't sound much like a spell to me. There was a sort of growling and grumbling, then a bell ringing and something that sounded like glass breaking.

"It's done," said Mum. "Open your eyes now!"

I opened mine, but Mum was still standing with hers squeezed shut.

"Well?" she said. "Did it work? I can't bear to look!"

"It's fine," I said. "The furniture is all back and everything looks okay." I looked out of the window. "And Aunt Martha is out on her front path scraping snow from it."

"I think," said Mum, "I'll just go and help her. We wouldn't want her to have an accident, would we? You make us some coffee, darling."

Now Mum can come pretty close to disaster on occasion, but sometimes she has a really good idea. When she came in from the garden with Aunt Martha, she was explaining her thinking.

"You see, I just don't think it's healthy for you to keep cleaning your house over and over again, Marthy," she was saying. "It's becoming an obsession. Why don't you come and clean our house once a week instead? That will keep you more than busy."

"It would be a life's work," said Aunt Martha drily, "but I suppose it is something I could do. I've never been any good at anything else, especially not magic, like you, Mary. I always rather wished I was, you know."

Mum looked astonished.

"When I think how I've envied your quiet, peaceful life," she said. "You know, magic is a bit of an obsession, too. Once you get started, you just can't stop. I guess we're more alike than I thought."

Aunt Martha is a lot happier these days. On Thursdays she comes around to

our house and works her own special
magic. It may not be as exciting as Mum's,
but it's a lot easier to live with!

The Bugle Bird

The bugle bird lived at the top of the tallest tree in the rain forest. All day long she sang: *bugle, bugle, bugle!* It was the kind of song that could get on your nerves if you heard it for more than two minutes. The other inhabitants of the rainforest had to listen to it hour after hour all day and every day. The snakes hated it. The tree frogs hated it. The sloths and the jaguars hated it. But most of all, the other birds hated it.

"It's the kind of thing that gives us a bad name," said an ancient parrot. "Even now that my hearing is not what it was, I can still hear that wretched bird bugling away up there. I'm sorry to talk so of one of my own kind, but I can't keep quiet any longer. I can't be the only one. What do you think, hummingbirds?"

The tiny, jewelled hummingbirds fluttered and danced to show that they agreed with the old parrot. A nearby sloth had something to say, too.

"I don't move about much," he mumbled from his upsidedown position, "so I can't even escape from that bird's silly song. The only thing I'm thankful for is that she doesn't sing at night.

"Perish the thought," purred the jaguar dangerously. "If she didn't live so high up, I would climb up there myself and ... shall we say, *deal* with the matter. But those small branches won't take my weight. Isn't there anyone else who could ... well, pay that bird a visit?"

Everyone turned to look at a very poisonous tree snake.

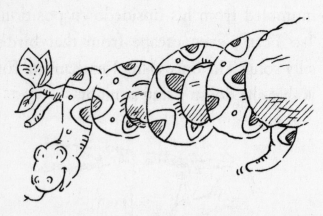

"Sssssee, I'm no assssassssin," he hissed. "Poissssoning someone you want to eat issss one thing, but I never have fanccccied feathersss and clawsssss."

It was a fair point. And the ancient parrot spoke for all of them when he said, "In any case, we really don't want any harm to come to the bugle bird. We just want her to be quiet."

Oh, and how they wanted her to be quiet! When the sun was shining brightly, casting splashes of colour through the leaves, the bugle bird sang. When the warm rain fell, day after day, the bugle bird sang. When the rain had stopped and little glittering raindrops shimmered on the leaves and trickled from petal to petal, the bugle bird sang. And she sang with all her heart.

"You would think," said the ancient parrot, "that we would get so used to the bugle bird's song that we wouldn't notice it after all this time. But it's such a terribly irritating noise, you just can't forget it's there. Don't you agree?"

The other creatures did agree. Some of them were even considering moving home to get away from the incessant bugling.

Then a small macaw said something interesting.

"I wonder," he chattered, "why she does it? I mean, we all make noises from time to time, but not *all* the time. Why on earth would a bird do that? It must be exhausting for her."

"That's a very good point," growled the jaguar, swinging his tail. "Perhaps it's her way of saying that she's ill or something —it certainly sounds like a creature in pain to me!"

No one seemed to know why bugle birds sang.

"One of us will just have to go and ask her," said the ancient parrot, looking around with his small bright eyes.

All of a sudden the other animals seemed to be fascinated by the trees and the leaves and the river. The jaguar even started humming softly and looking to see if his claws needed trimming.

The ancient parrot cleared his throat loudly.

"Look here," he said, "it can't be me because my joints are stiff and I'd never make it all the way to the top of the tree. It will have to be one of you young ones. How about it, macaws?"

But the macaws all shook their heads. The branches high up in the tree, they explained, were much too thin to take their weight. And their babies needed a great deal of attention just now.

"If a mere land animal could make a suggestion," the jaguar commented in silky tones, "what is stopping you from *flying* up to find that wretched bird?"

There was a pause. Then...

"Vultures!" cried the macaws.

"Turbulence!" hummed the little hummingbird.

"Spiders!" cried a younger parrot who particularly disliked the large and hairy variety that lived in the tree-tops.

"It seems," said the ancient parrot, "that no one wants to go and talk to the bugle bird. I'm sure she's charming. What is the matter with you all?"

"They're afraid she's as boring as her song," growled the jaguar, but so softly that no one else heard him.

Just then, there was a slithering in the branches and all the leaves shook.

"Ssssssend me!" hissed the tree snake, shaking his colourful coils.

The animals looked at him with some doubt. On the whole, they didn't like to encourage the snake to climb too high in the trees. Their nests and little ones were there, and whatever a snake may say about not liking feathers, you can't trust any creature when he's hungry.

"I rather think that those top branches would be too fragile for you, too," the ancient parrot explained. "And if you slip, you have no fingers or claws to catch on to the branches. No, we need a small, light, agile creature with a friendly face and a big smile."

"It's me! It's me!" shouted a tiny voice, and a green and red tree frog jumped up and down on a branch with glee, showing just how wide his smile could be.

That same afternoon, the little frog started hopping up the tree. He passed the sloths and the macaws. He waved cheerily to the parrots. He hopped up and up, higher than he had ever hopped before.

Pretty soon, the little frog needed a rest. He found a large and beautiful flower with its centre full of cold, clear water. Here, in the hottest part of the day, he splashed and cooled himself. Then he began climbing once more.

There was no difficulty about knowing which way to go. For one thing, he simply had to keep going up. For another, the bugle bird kept singing the whole time, and as the little frog climbed, her song grew louder and louder.

At last, just as the sun was beginnng to set, the little frog arrived at the branch directly underneath the bugle bird's nest. He decided to rest there for the night and talk to her in the morning when he was feeling fresh and friendly. In any case, as the light left the sky, the bugle bird stopped singing. The forest was silent except for the rustling of the leaves and the trickling of the river, far below.

The little frog made himself comfy on a large leaf and closed his eyes. But in another second he had opened them again. Quite close to him, someone was crying. Little broken-hearted sobs that brought tears to the frog's eyes wafted softly through the leaves. The frog listened hard. The longer he listened, the surer he was that the sobs were coming from the nest of the bugle bird, just above him.

The moon was high in the sky and the night was cool before the sobbing stopped and both the bugle bird and the little frog below her went to sleep at last.

Next morning, the little tree frog got down to business straight away. He hopped up on to the next branch and put his friendly face over the side of the nest "Good morning," he said politely, with his widest grin, "I am a little green tree frog. Do I have the honour of talking to the famous bugle bird?"

The bugle bird looked up, surprised.

"You do," she said. "How can I help you, little green tree frog?"

The frog coughed.

"Well, it's a slightly delicate matter," he began, "but all the creatures further down the tree have been very *struck* by your singing voice."

"Oh!" The bugle bird looked very much happier than she had been. "Have they? How wonderful! Would they like me to sing more often?"

"No! No!" The little frog feared that he would never be able to go home again if he allowed such a thing. "The thing is," he went on, "they have been so astonished by your stamina. They wonder how you manage to keep singing all the time as you do."

"Ah," sighed the bugle bird, "when you have a very good reason for singing, it is no trouble to do it all day long."

The little frog felt he was getting somewhere.

"And what, I wonder," he paused delicately, "would that reason be?"

For the first time, the bugle bird hesitated. She hung her head and sighed again—and again.

"That is a little embarrassing," she said at last. "I wish you would not ask me such a personal question."

The little frog put on his most sympathetic expression.

"Sometimes a trouble shared is a trouble halved," he said. It was something he had once heard the ancient parrot say.

The bugle bird sighed again. She was obviously keen to talk.

"Well," she said, "I sing to... The reason I sing is... That is, I sing because I hope to find... well, *another* bugle bird!"

"Another bugle bird?" the little frog shrieked in horror. One bugle bird was bad enough, surely? "But why?"

"Well..." If it were possible for birds to blush, that is just what the bugle bird would have done then. "I was hoping to find a ... well, a sweetheart," she said coyly, ruffling her feathers.

"Oh!" The little frog understood everything now. He looked at the bugle bird and felt his heart sink. She was not a beautiful bird. She had untidy brown feathers and a floppy kind of crest that fell into her eyes. She looked as interesting as her song, which was not saying much. The bugle bird had missed out on the brightly coloured plumage of the parrots and the macaws. She was nowhere near as neat and pretty as the hummingbirds. Now that he thought about it, he realized that he had no idea what a male bugle bird looked like, and he told the bugle bird so.

"Alas," said the bugle bird, "I have no idea myself. My dear father had a terrible accident before I was hatched, and my mother looked just as I do. She, too, did not have long to live. I'm afraid I know very little about bugle birds, although I am one."

She hunched her shoulders and hung her head.

The little frog frowned. He could think of nothing else to say, so he politely took his leave and hopped off down the tree. As he did so, he heard the bugle bird lift her voice in song once more.

It was much quicker going down. Shortly after noon, he reached the bottom of the tree, where the other animals were waiting eagerly for news.

It did not take the little frog long to tell them what he had found out.

"Hmm," said the ancient parrot. "I believe I did see a male bugle bird once. A rather flashy bird, with big blue feathers and an orange crest. But I haven't spotted one for years. I don't think much of our bugle bird's chances of finding a mate."

"I'm afraid my mission has been a terrible failure," said the little tree frog. "We are no further forward than we were before, are we?"

But the jaguar shifted his powerful shoulders restlessly and disagreed.

"I noticed something," he said, "while you were talking to the bugle bird this morning. I noticed something very interesting indeed."

"Hmm, I know what you mean," agreed the ancient parrot. "I noticed it, too. But I don't quite see what we can do about it."

"If there's anything I can do...?" squeaked the little frog, still feeling guilty about the failure of his mission.

"I think there is," smiled the jaguar. "What we both noticed was that while you were talking to the bugle bird, the bugle bird wasn't singing. It was bliss!"

The little green frog was not stupid. He saw at once what was being suggested and he began to shiver and shake.

"No!" he said. "I can't go and talk to her *all* the time. I simply can't!"

"Not all the time," said the parrot. "How about mornings only? We can all have a nice, peaceful morning, and that will give us the strength to put up with the bugle bird's singing in the afternoon."

The little frog felt bitter. He had done his best to help and now here he was, doomed for life to hear the moping of the bugle bird every morning. It was too much for a small tree frog to bear, and he said so.

The other animals looked a little bit ashamed of themselves.

"You are right, of course," said the ancient parrot. "I suppose we could organise some king of a rota."

There was some quarrelling and muttering, as there always is about rotas, and everyone felt it was unfair that there really was no way the jaguar or the sloth could make it to the top of the tree, but for the rest of the week, mornings in the rain forest were very, very peaceful.

The parrot chatted to the bugle bird about feathers and how to preen them. The bugle bird began to look a little tidier.

The macaws explained to her about beak care and nut-cracking. The bugle bird tried one or two delicacies other than caterpillars and insects A diet of creepy-crawlies is sure to make you depressed.

The tree frog took his turn as well. He found himself encouraging the bugle bird to take a little exercise. Personally, he

told her, he was in favour of hopping, but some creatures liked to run, or creep or, of course, fly.

The bugle bird looked thoughtful at this but refused to try in front of the little frog. Next time he visited, however, she shyly demonstrated that she had been practising a little dance.

The little green tree frog watched as the bugle bird flapped and flitted on the edge of her nest. She was really quite graceful, and when she had finished, the frog broke into genuine applause.

At the end of a month, the bugle bird was completely transformed. She was no longer miserable and lonely. She had friends from all parts of the forest and was a charming hostess to all her visitors. They in turn, and much to their surprise, found that they enjoyed their visits to the bugle bird. She was an asset to the forest.

"You know," said the ancient parrot, "now that I know the bugle bird as a friend, I find that I don't mind her bugling in the afternoons nearly so much."

The other animals agreed.

But only a few afternoons later, the animals were astonished to hear not one but two bugling tunes high up in the trees.

The ancient parrot shook his head. He couldn't believe what he was hearing. He hurried down to the sloth with a pleading look in his eyes. The sloth seemed to be sleeping, but he opened his eyes when he heard the fluttering of wings above him.

"Yes, I can hear it, too," he said. "There are two lots of bugling. What does it mean? Could it be an echo?"

"Of course not," purred the jaguar, making them both jump. "It's quite clear that the bugle bird has found a friend."

"I'm afraid you're right," agreed the ancient parrot. "And the noise is worse than it has ever been before. Yes, I am very much afraid you are right."

"Afraid? Why afraid?" the sloth queried lazily. "Surely it's a good thing if the poor creature has a friend?"

"Yes, of course," nodded the parrot. "But on the other claw…"

"I know what you mean," said the jaguar. "But we may be worrying about nothing. Only time will tell."

The tree snake, who slithered by just then, wanted to go and spy on the bugle bird to see who her friend was.

"It doesn't seem right to interrupt her if she has company," said the macaws primly. "We will all find out tomorrow."

The next morning, it was the little green tree frog's turn to visit the bugle bird, but as he hopped up through the branches, he became aware of other rustlings and flutterings among the leaves.

Just below the bugle bird's nest, it became clear that most of the animals who had visited in the past month had decided to make an extra special visit today. They balanced precariously on the thin branches around the bugle bird's home.

The bugle bird was preening her feathers and looking rather smug.

"My dear friend," began one of the macaws, "we couldn't help hearing an appalling... That is, yesterday afternoon some very, very beautiful singing wafted down to us through the trees."

"Ah, yes," said the bugle bird with a flutter of her feathers. "It would be my husband-to-be that you heard. He does have a remarkable voice, doesn't he?"

"Congratulations," said the parrot faintly. "I had no idea."

"No, it was all rather sudden," agreed the bugle bird. "But we are both very happy. If you stay a little longer, you will meet him, for he has just flown off to find me some fruit."

The other creatures did stay longer. The second bugle bird turned out to be a handsome fellow with handsome blue and orange tail feathers as well as a crest.

"I feel so fortunate to have met my beautiful wife-to-be," he said. "There are so few bugle birds in the forest, I thought that I would never meet another. Now we can settle down happily together."

With one voice, the visitors said one important word.

"*Where?*"

"Why, here, of course!" cried the first bugle bird. "I've been telling my dearest about all the good friends I have here. We wouldn't dream of settling in another part of the forest. We couldn't possibly leave all of you behind."

The ancient parrot gulped and said, "I'm sure there are other beautiful spots to settle. Wouldn't you like to make a new start to your new life? Much as we would miss you, of course."

The oldest macaw gulped and chirped, "Yesterday we found the perfect place to set up home. It had fruit and nuts and flowers and a beautiful stream. And," she lowered her voice, "there were no snakes or jaguars at all. I'd be very happy to show you, although naturally I don't really want you to leave."

The little tree frog tried as well.

"I do wonder," he said, "how safe this nest is for two fine birds. The branches here are very thin. Wouldn't it be better to build in a sturdier tree? I could help you look for one."

But the bugle birds would hear none of it.

"We want to stay here, where we met," they cooed, looking deeply into each other's eyes.

There was nothing else to be said.

For two weeks, the forest was filled with busy creatures preparing for the bugle birds' wedding. The smaller birds flittered here and there, gathering the most beautiful blossoms they could find. Others stored fruit and nuts for a great feast. The little green tree frog carried flat water-lily leaves up from the river for use as plates. Even the songbirds from the riverside practised a special wedding song.

At last everything was ready. In a large clearing, the wedding took place. Everyone was there, although most of the smaller creatures steered clear of the bright eyes of the jaguar. At the end of the ceremony, the songbirds sang, and the old parrot had tears running down his face.

"Weddings make me cry, too," said the little green frog kindly.

"It's not that," sniffed the parrot, shaking his head. "I'm crying because this is the last time we'll hear decent music in this part of the forest in my lifetime. From now on, we will hear nothing but bugling all day and every day."

The ancient parrot was right. The bugle birds flew away for a short honeymoon in the mountains. All was peaceful in the forest, but it was hard for the other animals to enjoy it. They knew that the return of the bugle birds was just a matter of time.

They were right. When the bugle birds returned, they sang and sang.

"Why did we ever think that one bugle bird was a problem?" groaned the macaws. "We didn't know when we were well off. Two is so much worse."

"We don't even get a gap between songs, if you can call them that," sighed the frog. "When one isn't singing, the other one is. I'm very fond of the bugle bird, although I don't see so much of her these days, but her singing is just awful. Why didn't we teach her to sing instead of all those dancing and preening and feeding lessons? It's all our fault!"

The tree snakes and the jaguar even began discussing bugle-bird-removal plans again, but nothing came of it.

Then, one fine morning when the forest steamed gently in the heat, the old parrot woke up feeling brighter and more energetic than usual.

"I don't know what it is," he said, "but I feel twenty years younger."

"I know what you mean," squawked a passing macaw. "It must be the time of the year."

The jaguar, prowling beneath their branches, had more interesting news.

"It isn't the time of the year," he growled. "It's something else. Listen!"

The birds listened.

"I don't hear anything," said the parrot, putting his head on one side.

"Neither do we," agreed the bright-eyed macaws, waggling their beaks.

"Precisely," purred the jaguar, and he strolled off through the trees making no sound as his feet padded over the moss.

Within seconds, the message had swept around the forest. The creatures gathered around a low tree, unable to believe their ears.

"There hasn't been a single bit of bugling since dawn," said the tree frog. "I can't understand it at all."

"They may have gone on holiday," the tree snake suggested.

Everyone turned to look at him, a terrible suspicion forming in their minds.

"They might be ill," said the parrot with a sharp glance at the snake. "Or worse. We will have to go and see."

Once again, the animals hopped and flittered and slithered and crept up into the highest branches of the tallest tree. They moved as quietly as they could, but even so there was a good deal of rustling and creaking as the leaves shook and the tree swayed.

Just below the bugle birds' nest, the animals paused awkwardly.

"I'm frightened to look," said the little green tree frog.

"*Sssssshhhhhhhhh!*" came a voice from above. "Please be quiet! I've only just go these little ones to sleep, and I don't want to disturb them. Can't you rustle a little more quietly?"

One by one, the forest creatures peeped over the edge of the nest. The bugle birds were sitting proudly in their home, which had been considerably enlarged in the past few months. Around them huddled six little bugle chicks, with their eyes closed.

"Aaah!" sighed the parrot and the macaws and the frog. "How beautiful they are! You must be very proud."

The animals stayed a few minutes to congratulate the bugle bird and admire her babies, then they headed back down the tree.

"Are you thinking what I am?" the parrot asked the little green frog.

"Yes," said the frog. "I'll meet you in the clearing in half an hour."

And that is why, later that day, you would have seen a curious sight. A parrot, several macaws, four humming birds, two snakes, a sloth, a jaguar and a little green tree frog set off together to find a new home along the river.

After all, one bugle bird's singing is hard to bear. Two bugle birds are worse. But eight bugle birds?